D0935958

The
Man-Eaters of Cascalon

The
Man-Eaters of Cascalon

GENE LANCOUR

DOUBLEDAY & COMPANY, INC.

GARDEN CITY, NEW YORK

1979

For Lonna:

"Autumn is a time of fading, where light,
Color, and hot laughing joy turn somber
In swift running days to a failing year—
Though I shall feel again its cooling bite
As short days flow by in countless number
Always, Love, I shall also feel you near."

For you, this first of many more. . . .

Library of Congress Cataloging in Publication Data

Lancour, Gene.
The man-eaters of Cascalon.

I. Title.
PZ4.L245Man [PS3562.A467] 813'.5'4 5
ISBN: 0-385-13565-3
Library of Congress Catalog Card Number 78-68352

I

It was the same monstrous sow bear.

Dirshan, his breath a frosty cloud that swirled around his bent form, rose from his crouching position to stand erect. The carcass of the sow's last kill—the not-quite frozen remains of a much-chewed four-hundred-pound black bear—lay at his feet. It had delayed for too long its entry into the winter den. Of its killers, nothing remained but tracks in the light powder of two-inch snow; one set, those of the sow, broader than his hand was long, the other set much smaller and probably those of the yearling cub which Dirshan knew to be traveling with her. Both sets led upward and across a tiny barren field, then through a defile between two funneling walls, and disappeared.

But they would be back. There was still plenty of meat left on the carcass. It was already too late in the season and they were too high to find another kill before denning up for the cold ahead. Dirshan bent down for one more look at the larger track beside his booted foot, looking closely at the deformed toe to make sure it was that of the beast he had tracked for the last tenday. Once sure, he retraced his steps back into the mixed larch and brush which fringed the lower edge of the field. He would be waiting when they next came to feed. And this time it would be the sow and not his older brother which would bleed its life out in the snow.

Once into the trees, Dirshan unslung his pack and weapons, then removed the small battle-ax from his belt and set about building a blind. He had hunted these mountains much in his youth. He knew that while bears' sight was not very keen they relied much on both smell and hearing. Was it not said in the manhood ceremony of the Bear clan during his youth—in that curious fusion of the old beliefs and the newer, stronger faith in Rema—"May Rema give him the strength and the cunning of the bear"? In one respect Dirshan was fortunate; the wind was funneled off the tops of the range before him and through the defile. It would be over the kill and in his face.

He worked swiftly. Already in this hunt he had made three blinds: two baited with fish taken from the still-running streams over the lower hills and once over a day-old kill. Only once had the bears come in, but he had not had a shot with the bow he carried. The wind had shifted; and first the sow and then her cub had winded him, both departing with the soft, uncanny silence of the large beast in dense brush. He had feared that they would both circle and come at him from behind; a talent at which this sow was reputed to be adept, but it was not so. Already the pressure of denning was upon them; Dirshan felt that it was only the lack of a blizzard which had kept them from doing so. The huge brown-and-white mottled bears of the highlands in the Garmaliki Range, of which these were two, denned only during that time, knowing by some uncanny method that this would cover their tracks. Yet winter was already spreading its snow deeper on the frowning mass of rock above and around him. Now would be the last time to take the sow—before spring broke the cold's grip. With Rema's help, the she-bear would fall on this spot.

Once the blind was completed, Dirshan gathered up his goods and relaxed under it; the small bow to one side and three crested shafts in easy reach. The overcast sky provided only a diffused, cold light; the wind of late afternoon brought the yelps and howls of scavengers from the near distance. Dirshan had measured with his eye the five-rod distance from his blind to the bait. Now he would relax. He would easily hear them before they came in, and he needed the rest. He had walked the entire day. Bears move swiftly when they know they are pursued.

Giving minimal attention to the whiteness around him, Dirshan let his thoughts roam, eddying through the past like the light flakes of snow which had slowly begun to fall. His mind quickly reviewed the past three moons which had ultimately led him to this final drama in ice and snow.

The late summer rains dripped and fell from the eaves in the imperial city of Alithar, making mock of the stones of man and the Empire's recent victory over both League and bad odds to a triumph on the heaving Heclos. Dirshan was sitting beneath one of the outside porticoes of the Pillars, the residence of the Family which ruled Alithar and the Empire. He watched as the gray mist fell past and down to the lower city. Behind him, the silent tread of the servant was respect itself, but Dirshan had heard him come out through the doors at the other end and awaited his coming. This same silent tread and self-effacing character of servants in the Pillars was only one more of the irritations which disturbed him about Alithar; as did the colorful throngs in the city below and the tame blandness which he saw in the too-civilized. That others he knew did not find it so served only to further irk him in his black moods. He wished himself ahorse, afield, and far away.

The servant came into his field of vision, but before he had a chance to mutter the traditional "Rema be with you, lord," Dirshan had turned. Looking down on him from his six-foot five-inch height, Dirshan said, "What is it you want? I asked not to be disturbed." He was in a very black mood.

The servant was somewhat disconcerted—but not unduly—by Dirshan's tone. His family had served the rulers of Alithar for ten generations, and Dirshan's reputation for uncouthness was as noted in the Pillars as were his victories in the Empire's name. As far as he was concerned, both could be safely ignored. "A messenger has come to the lower gate and requests audience with you. He is ragged and dirty, as if from much travel. He would not have been admitted at all except he claimed knowledge and will not be persuaded to relay his message through the regular channels. His only words are 'Tell the Lord Dirshan that one of the Hawk clan has a message.' He refuses to say more. Also, he knocked down one of the guards when they made an attempt to remove him." The man lapsed into silence.

Dirshan had a momentary urge to also knock someone down —this time a supercilious servant. He was prevented by the surge of joy the man's news had given him. The messenger down below would be from his old homeland; of that he was sure. "I will see this one in my rooms, immediately!"

The servant went to turn away. Dirshan called after him, "And if any more violence is offered him, I will have a head. Depend on it." The servant scurried away. Dirshan's reputation also held an element of casual violence.

While waiting for this messenger from his past, Dirshan made his way swiftly to his rooms; once there, he stripped off his robes and put on a pair of leather breeks. A polished steel mirror on one wall returned a wavering reflection of his form, his head cut off because it had been made to conform to the smaller stature of the born members of the Family. His iron-gray body hair and the seamed scars with their pink ridges were surface blemishes on the muscled body, the flesh stretched taut and hard over his form. High on the left shoulder was the tiny figure of a blue hawk in full flight; its form indistinct now. It was over twenty cycles ago that it had been put there on his being declared a man of the clan. He had just finished rinsing his face in cold water when there came a discreet knock on the marblewood door.

"Enter!" he bellowed, turning to greet his visitor.

The one who entered was young; perhaps only eighteen or twenty cycles had passed since his birth. He had been disarmed and was partially followed into the room by two guards. Dirshan waved them out without a word as he looked over the visitor. He was almost as tall as Dirshan, but his iron-gray hair and the level gaze of his eyes told more than his speech that he was a barbarian. Only the city-bred practiced the money-making art of deception. He wore leather, much stained and worn. An empty sheath for a short sword hung at his belt. Dirshan smiled and walked forward to clasp arms, saying in his native tongue, "And does the Hawk clan prosper in the vales below the Hasiditsi, clan brother?"

To Dirshan's surprise, the other did not immediately answer. He only fell to his knees and touched his head to the thick carpet. "Aieee!" he keened. "I give fealty and obedience to the chief of my clan! May the hawk our brother give him speed and the keen sight, and may his face shine on the smallest of his brothers!" He remained on his knees, his eyes not above Dirshan's ankles.

"Rise," Dirshan commanded, not expecting this greeting and worried over what it portended. "What is this you speak of? Does not Latran, my father, still hold the vales of the Hawk? Rise, I said, and speak of these things."

The other rose to his feet, his entire attitude telling both of his respect for Dirshan and a slight fear. "I bear word of sorrow for your house, clan father," he said, the words rushing out. "I am called Ke'in, son of Penmal, whose strength and counsels were high in the clan. Thy father was taken and is now known dead. So, too, is thy brother Shaget, taken by the great sow bear who has been ravaging the steads on the higher vales." There was a slight catch in his voice. "He died in saving the lives of two; this unworthy one now owes your house a life. I was sent by the Hawks to bid your return, for news of thy fame and victories have come on the wind over the mountain. It was deemed that only you could return and send these evils which have come to the tribe Garazi and the twelve clans back to their ancient lairs.

"I have traveled for three moons in search of you. The Worlde is wider than I had known. I had never been beyond the vales and had not seen service with the Order. Both my elder brothers died for Rema. Only I am left of my house."

Dirshan motioned him to a seat on one of the heavily cushioned divans which littered the room, a little confused by the sudden news. A hidden sorrow had come into his heart on the death of his father and brother. They had not been close, and he had left to join the Order early in his youth, but his family was the source of his strength. "Begin from the start and leave nothing out. First: of my father. Taken by whom, and when?"

"This past cycle has been one of great portent. War has

risen and fallen between Empire and League. The snows fell early last season, and continued long on the slopes. A great fire was seen in the sky. I was not privileged to the decisions made in the Great Council, but as you know, even before you left to go in the ranks of the Order, many still had not taken to the oath of the Shrine and faith in Rema. They still followed the old ways and belief in the clan gods before the tribe; and the Shrine, if at all, last. The two main clans which stood in the old beliefs were those of the Bear and the Badger, but others agreed and resented the loss of the old ways. But thy father and others dominated the Great Council, and the clans they led in turn made the tribe follow the old ways only in name, not in fact. Ever this has been a source of friction, for many did not like the colorless face of the new when the old gods still roamed the highlands for all to see.

"Wait!" Ke'in exclaimed, reading Dirshan's look. "I am of thy clan"—he pulled up his sleeve to expose a tiny blue hawk that shone with its relative newness—"but I still cleave to the Shrine. We have furnished many for the wars in the east. You are not the only one not to return to thy birthplace.

"It was a little over ten cycles ago that Aliffa, who was of the Bear clan, left his father's hearth and declared himself bandit. He took as his seat one of the mountain walls under the knee-caps of Muraaz, and built there a hold. Since that time all landless and clanless men have flocked to him, for he will take anyone who declares against the Shrine and the men who fight for it. At first he restricted himself only to raids against the east, and there was only an occasional foray on a small band of the Shrine who chanced his way. With war here in the north, many of the Order had been withdrawn, deeming that their place lay with city rather than the Shrine. So the activities of Aliffa were tolerated both by the Great Council and the Chapter House in Anshan, for many argued that there should always be a place for those who do not believe or have no recourse to their clan.

"Such it remained until the beginning of this last cycle. Then came these portents, and the gathering war to the north recalled many who had kept back the pressure from the east and Cascalon on the Black Meer. Aliffa then sent heralds through all the clans, saying that the Shrine was no more and it was time for the Garazi to return to their own. Many heard this at the Great Meet and agreed, especially since the portents seemed to indicate some change in the winds of the Worlde. A great sow bear began to ravage the highland steads, and Aliffa of the Bear clan, claimed this as evidence that the old gods were returning. Men began to gather from all the clans to Aliffa's hold, and by this increase in strength increased his boldness. Raiding has again come to the mountains—only this time he raids against both the Order and those who oppose him."

While the messenger paused to gain breath, Dirshan turned over in his mind the facts he knew of the northern war which dovetailed with Ke'in's tale. He had been instrumental in defeating the latest attack on the Empire and knew that it had resulted in a withdrawal of the Order from the frontiers. He poured them both a draught of wine, and motioned for Ke'in to drink his. "Go on. What happened to my father?"

"It was finally decided that some effort would have to be made to dissuade Aliffa from his madness, for it was widely known that neither the Order nor those in Anshan would tamely submit to renewed raiding. They would rightly blame *all* the clans. Truce was declared and thy father and some others went up to Aliffa's hold to make parley before those of the Order or Anshan would come to make all suffer. Aliffa took them all and hanged them, disemboweled, from the cliff of his hold. He sent back word that this would be the fate of all who disputed the old gods and still kept to the false faith of Rema.

"With thy father dead, the old custom was followed, and thy brother Shaget was declared in his place. By this time Aliffa had assumed control of the Bear clan; so that your brother and the clan leader of the Deer, who had also suffered from his insolence, called feud, hoping to unite the others into a war to destroy him and his hold. Before this was done, it was deemed necessary to first eliminate the sow bear which had been at work in the highlands, for Aliffa claimed that this was proof that the old gods still lived. Your brother set out to do this. We failed." Defeat was heavy in his voice. "Thy brother died as he had lived, foremost in valor and the first to fall. He took the sow's ear, but in trying to save myself and another with us, was killed. We came down from the highlands, but there was dismay through all the clans. None of thy house was left except your brother's two sons—six and nine cycles—and they had not yet undergone the tests for manhood. All this was viewed by the rest of the clans as a portent of defeat should any rise against Aliffa. The attempt to take his hold was put off and is now abandoned. He is too strong, it is said, and has one of the old gods to champion his right. And I cannot say that it may not be true, for the sow is a demon. I have seen her, and she has the cunning and deceit of a god.

"It was even whispered that Aliffa had allied himself with the animals from the east—the eaters-of-the-dead, the Ayal from Cascalon. Before I left, they had even raided unto Anshan!

"War has come unto the vales of thy home. The other members of the clan took counsel among themselves and decided to send a messenger to find you, if that were possible. Your fame has echoed through the hills. It was thought that only your great power could prevent the bloodshed which is sure to follow." His voice was gloomy and presaged doom. "Those of Anshan have already closed the Great Fair and vowed to crush the clans utterly while we fight among ourselves."

Dirshan began to pace, his feet making slight scuffling noises as they crossed the thick carpets which littered the floor. Finally he stopped in front of Ke'in. "I hear the call of our clan and my people. But my work here is not yet finished; the war with the League awaits only inattention for it to flare anew. And yet"—a wave of homesickness passed over him, a vision of the clean space and towering heights of the great Garmaliki Range above him as he and his brother hunted in the upper vales of the mountains—"there is nothing which cannot be completed without me. To get away . . ." He did not finish the sentence, for suddenly it seemed that here was his way to remove himself from the city that was slowly killing his spirit.

"Gett!" he suddenly shouted, almost startling the youth who was watching him. The door opened to admit one of the servants.

"Your wish?" he asked, looking at the divan and the visitor.

"Where is that misbegotten son of a whore Gett, who is supposed to attend me?" Dirshan bellowed.

"I know not, lord. Perhaps in the lower city . . ." His voice trailed off. The antics of Dirshan's companion and sometime servant were one of the continuing scandals of the Pillars.

"Have him found. Now!" Dirshan said flatly, the note in his voice a warning to speed. "And have the order passed that I want a galley, ready and docked at Jien for the morning tide. I leave Alithar tonight." The servant scurried away to do his bidding. Dirshan walked over to where the cut crystal of the wine flagon transmitted the wan light from the window into a red reflection on the marble table. "To the clan," he said as he raised the glass he filled, Ke'in hastily following. "Go into the other room and get some rest on the bed there. We sail on the morrow." Both drained their glasses. Without further word, Ke'in did as he was bid. He was tired, and the wishes of his clan chief had echoed his own desires.

And it was done as Dirshan had commanded. Before midday next, the galley was coasting south over the Heclos. Its captain did Dirshan's bidding not only because he was an appointed member of the Family that ruled Alithar, but also he was known as the man who had won the recent war with the League. It was only when the three travelers—Ke'in, Dirshan, and his servant/companion Gett—had finally gone hull down from the sight of Jien, though not from the vast assemblage of shipping which surrounded the port, did Dirshan finally relax. He could almost feel the weight of civilization lift from his shoulders, the dead conventions of an Empire which he had defended but never really felt comfortable with. His spirit expanded.

Not that there had not been complications in Dirshan's leaving. They ranged from his supposed responsibilities in the final pacification of the League forces which still resisted the downfall of Sart, the League capital, to the entreaties of the other members of the Family that he should wait and so gather whatever forces his name and reputation could command. He refused them all, claiming only a galley for transportation and gold, refusing even a letter to the empire of Anshan, the land to the southwest of his homeland. Only to Gett had he given the choice of remaining or following him to this new war. The little man paused only a moment before replying, "I'll take this voyage with you. I'm running out of fleshpots in the lower city anyhow, mate, and this Pillars stifles me!"

And so, while Gett, at Dirshan's insistence, spent the voyage with Ke'in learning the language, Dirshan occupied his time in weapons practice. The short, two-foot anlace came easily back into his grasp, as did the small and handy ax he had taken to carrying with it. Akamatoth, the long sacrificial knife whose blade once took lives for a god and now did the same for Dirshan, hung beside it. Only these and sometimes a small bow did he carry into battle, though the mail shirt which fitted him like a second skin was proof against even the heaviest of swords. It, too, had been a gift; its only mate hung in the old room of the Pillars, worn once by the founder of the Empire and there preserved with his body in ancient state. As the days and the leagues passed by, Dirshan's body again became taut; the fighting machine which had been dulled by some time of city life now came back to its perfection. That journey over the Heclos took a moon, with stops for provisions. It was night when they finally came to the southern shore and the bend in the great trail that led south.

As the galley had followed the coastline of the Heclos, the mountains which fringed its western shore had finally receded, only to curve back again as they coasted the southern shore. Only two passes pierced that massif. One, hard behind the

League city of Gades, led directly overland through the passes to the capital of Anshan, a land region which took its name, as did Alithar, from the leading city. From Gades another trail followed the southern shore of the Heclos between the sea and the Garmaliki Range to the south, until it finally turned south to cross at the second pass. The pass itself was called in the language of Dirshan's people Hasiditsi or "Horse-breaker" because of the narrow paths and the dangerous slides. On the other side of the high-banked peaks and their white, sun-gilded tops was the beginnings of Dirshan's homeland.

Dirshan dismissed the galley and they set their faces south; only Gett looked at the departing ship with some wistfulness. He was from Sart, that bare knowledge alone said he was a man of the sea. He preferred a slippery deck to sliding stones covered with ice. Though he followed Dirshan with his heart, his head told him to remain on the water. At the first inn on the road, they procured horses and provisions; and there Dirshan, with some guile, declared their destination as Anshan, back on the trail toward Gades. The hillmen who inhabited this side of the range had little to sustain them except plunder. A small party was fit meat—like a herd of deer sent by the gods.

They cleared the pass in three days, killing only one horse and three hillmen in the process. Once on the other side and below the snow line, Dirshan had them set up camp. The trail here came down from the pass and then branched into two narrow dirt trails: one going east, into the land of Dirshan's tribe, the other west, on to Anshan and its borders. All three sat on a knoll which overlooked this branching, the towering peaks as a backdrop behind them and the plains gradually opening out into the near and far distance.

Ke'in spoke first. "Over four moons have sought the endless rim of the Worlde since I last saw any of our clan. We know not what may have taken place. Aliffa may have already taken all."

"I think not," Dirshan had said then. "There is some hope left; others will be of your mind. As I remember, the closest stead of our own clan lies no more than five leagues east. There," he pointed with his fingers. "Is that right?"

"No," Ke'in replied. "Even before I left, most of the steads closer to the eastern border of Anshan had been deserted. Their people have retreated deeper into the hills with the flocks, knowing that the Anshani would not take long to retaliate once Aliffa began raiding. It will take time to find them, and then more time to see if any still oppose Aliffa. The borders of Anshan," he motioned to the right, or east, "lie at most fifteen leagues away. I would not be surprised if some of their parties are even now scouring the hills. We must be careful."

"You will have to go in search of them. Say nothing of my return except to those of our clan, and only to those you know. It is two days past since the moon has hidden its face in darkness. By the time of the full moon, I will meet with you here, with as many of our clan as you can find. Bring horses and provisions and as much knowledge as you can obtain. Build camp in the hidden vale we passed afore, the one I mentioned. I want to know especially if any of the Anshani are operating in the mountains, and where."

"I hear you, O Hawk," Ke'in had answered formally. "And you?"

"We go to take this bear that slew my brother. I would see if this is a god. I think not. Gods do not die."

Ke'in accepted this with bowed head. Gett looked at Dirshan sourly. He anticipated a long walk through these mountains, with some danger and little drink.

He was not wrong.

It took a tenday for Gett and Dirshan to skirt the far eastern upper edge of the tree line, looking for the spoor of the two bears. They carefully avoided the settled steads, and in that time came upon only three solitary people: two boys and an old man, tending a flock late in this season. The last of these finally gave them the information which Dirshan had been seeking. Before the day was finished, he had discovered the fresh track of the two bears. Taking one horse and enough food to last him through the hunt, he made a permanant camp and left Gett in charge of it. When Gett made complaint, voicing his opposition to Dirshan's fighting two bears single-handed, Dirshan had told him, "It is a matter of honor. Not only for my brother, but also for its importance to the tribe. If I do not return within a tenday, go back and tell Ke'in. Under no circumstances try to follow me. Should the bear win, it is of no purpose for both to die." He said no more and disappeared under the trees.

In three days the horse was dead, its leg broken in a pothole as they forded a rushing stream. Dirshan cut its throat and used the carcass for bait, but the bear which came in to take it was not the one he sought. He left it to its meal and passed on, always searching for the pair of animals. Only once in the long trek did he get close enough to see the sow, up above on a ridge line as she passed over it. But as winter deepened he drew ever closer. Soon, very soon . . .

It was a deep, snuffling noise which warned him. The snow had stopped as the light faded, coating everything with a thin blanket of whiteness that reflected the remaining daylight and gave everything a brightness that belied the time. Dirshan came out of his reverie, now alert but completely immobile as he waited for the bears to come in. Then the snuffling came again—the sound of a bear as it sniffed the air for danger.

Suddenly the huge form was before him, the white-and-brown mottled hide moving with the swiftness of a large beast in its natural home. Dirshan clearly saw the huge animal as the sow sniffed the air, the ragged tear where an ear had been telling him that this was indeed the one he sought. The wind came into his face and brought him the rank odor of the sow. The cub was not with her, but he assumed that it was off foraging for itself somewhere. Just as well—it was only the sow he wanted. She lumbered quietly across the fallen snow, quiet as death moving up to the blooded carcass. Dirshan began to ease his bow out from under the hide covering, his hands stinging as the cold air bit into them. The sow halted suddenly a rod beyond the kill. Dirshan froze, straining to control his breath as the surge of adrenaline sped through his system. Nine hundredweight of bone and muscle quested the air, seeming to sense that something was wrong. Then she started forward again, more slowly, as Dirshan finished easing the bow out. He nocked an arrow, his movements slow and unhurried as the crunch of snow from her movements came clearly to him.

The bow was half-drawn to his lip when there was a low, throaty growl from his right. Dirshan's swift glance immediately told him what had happened. While he had been fixedly watching the sow, her cub had come in behind him and now stood, swaying, only five feet from his left side. The sudden snap of his head to look must have frightened it, for the low growl suddenly changed to a high-pitched whine as it began to back out and away from his blind.

Out of the corner of his eye, Dirshan saw the immediate result. A bellow came from the sow as she leaped the vast carcass before her and charged. The words of his now-dead father came to his mind. He had made the mistake which he had been warned of so many cycles ago: "Never get between a sow and her cub!" Latran had warned. "You'll have to kill her to stop her or she'll kill you!"

II

Under the circumstances, Dirshan had no alternatives.

With a rolling dive, he dropped the now-useless bow and leaped out of the blind, as chance would have it almost directly on top of the still-squealing cub. It scrambled out of his way. A small tangle of beaten furze broke the rush of Dirshan's fall. Rolling on one shoulder, he stood erect, his hand gripping the tiny ax which he had used to build the blind. In the few seconds remaining, he had but time for a mumbled prayer to Rema before the bear was on him.

In his youth and in the company of his father, Dirshan had hunted many bears. He knew it would be useless for him to run. He knew that a charging bear could outrun a deer within fifty rods and make less noise doing it than the deer's attempting to escape. He would have to stand his ground. There was a chance that the sow would ignore him and take after the still-fleeing cub, whose progress Dirshan could hear somewhere off to his right. But that was not to be. With a rending crash, the sow came right through the broken brush he had used as a blind.

Spotting him, the sow rose to her hind legs and growled a challenge. One paw flicked out and scored four furrows in the deep bark of the tree beside her, fully a foot over the top of Dirshan's head. Small hot eyes glared at him out of the mottled brown-and-white face. She dropped back on all fours, swaying ponderously from side to side and swinging her head. Dirshan knew what she was doing: The sow was attempting to locate him before charging. He did not wait.

With the war cry RE-MA! RE-MA! RE-MA! echoing in the

air, Dirshan charged the bear instead. A rumbling cry—almost
a scream—came from her throat as she did likewise, rising up
on her haunches as they came together. Dirshan did not enter
that fatal embrace. He darted to one side at the last moment.
The tiny ax flickered and spun in the air, the blade catching
the wan light for a moment before the short arcing stroke
ended in the sow's left shoulder joint. A gout of blood foun-
tained, proving that he had cut at least one artery, but the
blade locked in the wound as the bear turned. The force of
that blow and the bear's response wrenched the haft of the ax
from his hand.

As he tried to hold on, he was pulled off balance. The beast's
paw flickered out and grazed his arm. The numbing force of
the impact sent him spinning away to crash into the trunk of a
larch and then fall to the ground, stunned. The harsh bellow of
the wounded animal rang in the trees as she pulled and tore at
the blade which had slashed her. Dirshan watched dazedly as
the sow dropped on all fours, favoring the wounded side, and
tore about in a circle attempting to rid herself of the buried
blade. Grunts and howls rang through the branches as she momentarily forgot him in her pain.

But Dirshan knew that this forgetfulness would not last for
long. The beast was wounded, but far from dead. As she swung
around, slashing and tearing at anything within reach, he
scuffled backward behind the tree against which he had been
hurled. A sudden crack! told of a four-inch tree broken off short
by the violence of the bear's swings. The blind with its dropped
bow was ten feet in front of him, the sow to its left about five
feet. Dirshan judged his chances. There was no choice. He
would have to attempt it if he wanted to leave the clearing
alive.

As the bear continued to turn in a circle and tug at the haft
of the ax with her teeth, Dirshan waited for his opportunity.
With one leap he made the scanty protection of the blind and
scooped up the bow. Yet the sow had seen his movement even
in the failing light. She immediately seemed to remember him
as the cause of her pain. A roaring challenge announced that

she would follow him, crashing into a tree in her fury and bulling it over as she came to take him.

There would only be time for one shot—this Dirshan knew. He snatched up one of the arrows which lay on the trampled snow and shakily fitted it to the string. The nock was drawn to his lips and the whetted edge of the broadhead rested on his fist when, with one leap, she cleared the brush and entered the blind to face him. He released the arrow just as she came down within the blind.

It was not a killing shot. The arrow hit the moving bear and sank its shaft to the fletching in her massive chest, almost directly at the point where the collarbones joined. In that instant, there was a moment of clarity which often came to Dirshan in a battle. He was suddenly aware of the harsh taste and stench of fear in the air, mingled with the rank odor of the beast before him. His breath and the sow's were visible mists between them, both glowing in the failing light. For that one instant, she glared at him. Dirshan had the clear feeling that the sow knew she was dead, but that she would take him along to whatever awaited her after her passing. Somehow in her thrashing she had tossed the ax, and blood now flowed from the gaping wound in her shoulder. He knew that before long she would bleed to death, though he had seen a heart-shot bear run for an hour without stopping.

Then the instant of calm was wiped away. With another roar, the sow was upon him.

In an instant of fury, Dirshan barely had time to draw Aka-matoth, the ancient sacrificial knife, before she was upon him. The force of that shock knocked him completely backward, and he slid through the front of the wrecked blind out into the little field, his back sliding on the thin film of new-fallen snow. The sow's stench and the odor of newly spilt blood filled the air around him as the beast followed, still favoring her side. He had only enough time to roll and hunch his back before she stood above him.

The gift of ancient mail saved his life. Worn underneath his jerkin of untanned hide, it frustrated the sow's rending teeth worrying at his shoulder. The animal's vast weight was now in the center of his back, holding him down, as she tore at him, effectively pinning his knife hand to the center of his stomach and the wet snow beneath. Dirshan's only concern at that moment was to protect his head and neck. If the sow gained purchase, she would snap his spine. Instead of resisting her, he lay inert, letting her work out her fury on mail forged to take more punishment than she could give.

A sudden wrenching pain behind his left shoulder told him that she had found some purchase. He realized that he could no longer lie there, hoping that sooner or later the beast would back off for an attack at a better angle. As the massive jaws ground together, he twisted and turned beneath her, snaking out his knife hand. It was almost paralyzed now, both from cold and the angle; but once he had it free, he drew his arm forward to the position of the vast paw whose claws were inches from his face. With a quick slicing motion, he tore at the tendon behind the shaggy wrist joint, cutting again and again as the fetid breath of the sow rasped in his face. There was a sudden parting beneath the blade. With another roar that almost deafened him, the bear released her hold and backed off, bellowing her defiance.

Dirshan scrambled to his knees, facing the beast which now backed off about ten feet and began to circle him. Judging solely by her roars, he assumed that she was looking for another opening and he struggled to his feet to receive it, unsteady with pain a burning brand down his left side.

She rushed again. But this was a mere feint. Instead of crashing into him again, this time surely finishing one or the other, she lumbered past by at least a yard and headed across the barren field toward the narrow defile through which she had entered. The sow limped on both sides, leaving great blotches of gore on the white snow, visible even in the faint light that remained. Dirshan simply fell to his knees and watched her depart. Only Rema knew how close he was to death.

The crystal and jet sprays that were night and stars had fully appeared before he roused himself from his stupor. Death was very near. He could feel it in the cold, then warm fingers that crossed his ripped neck, and again in the frozen mantle of blood—either his or the sow's—which coated his back. Willing himself to his feet, he stumbled over what was left of the blind and began to scratch in the debris for his pack. He must have fire soon, or the howling wolves would have more than one carcass to pick at this night.

With one numb arm, he was handicapped in trying to strike the tinder in the tiny metal box, but he finally wedged it between his wet, unfeeling knees and got it to glow. The small pile of wet, broken brush which he managed to drag together proved difficult to light, but his prayers were answered as a tiny tongue of flame danced into existence and was soon fanned into a crackling blaze that grew as he piled on more and more of the broken branches. Several handfuls of snow quenched his thirst as he moved as close to the fire as possible, crisping one side and then the other. Once the blood was again liquid, he explored the ragged wounds in his neck and shoulder. He had the momentary satisfaction of finding that the ancient mail had indeed held; what wounds he had were at the junction of the collar, where the sow had managed to insert her fangs beneath it. That was bad enough—four ragged wounds and one gash that already had begun to stiffen his side—but they had ceased to bleed heavily and now oozed but little blood.

As night gathered into darkness, he busied himself with building a crude shelter with poles and his ground cloth, angling it so that the heat of the fire was on his back. Another half hour was spent in retrieving what was left of his gear, though he could not find the ax which had given such pain to the bear. That would wait until the cold dawn, when he would track the dying beast.

Though tired, sore, and wounded, Dirshan would have to track the animal. Though the rapidly clouding sky foretold snow, Dirshan hoped that it would not come and obliterate the tracks before he could follow. Though the three wounds which Dirshan knew the sow now had were serious, he had hunted enough bear to know that did not mean she would die. Bears were notorious for their strength and cunning. He himself had seen one at a distance remove an arrow dangling from one haunch, and like a man, patch the wound with mud from a stream bank. Though it would take much more than mud to patch the wound where the ax had cut into her and he was fairly sure by the frothing quality of some of the blood around the blind that the arrow had pierced at least one lung. But only Rema knew what would happen were the sow permitted to lie up in some covert and regain her strength. Bears were known to circle around and follow an antagonist, finishing the hunter off when he least expected it. No, either this sow would die, or he would not leave the highlands.

The weather held through the night as Dirshan alternated between drowsing to ease the pain of his wounds and rousing to throw more faggots on the fire. The howl of wolves came close sometime before dawn and then stopped, drawn both by the scent of blood and the carcass which lay just outside the circle of firelight. Several times Dirshan came awake to see yellow eyes that glared balefully at him from across the firelight; but they feared the flame and came no closer. When the sun finally gilded the peaks high around him, he felt he had won the victory simply because he was alive, even if stiff.

His leathers were caked with blood but at least dry. He methodically chewed and swallowed the dry travel rations which were all he had left as food, delicious despite the crumbly texture and smoked taste of the dried meat. He thoroughly searched the scene of combat until he found the tiny ax, its blade now notched. Then, after tying up his one bad arm to ease it, he gathered up his pack and began to track the sow. He needed her head and claws—this was the only way he could prove she had died.

The sow's trail was not hard to follow, though it led through tough and difficult country. The light cover of new snow and absence of wind aided him, as did the fact that she neither swerved nor deviated from the straight path that paralleled the tree line. At one time she was joined by the cub, and for a while they traveled together. Then he came to a spot where they split apart again. This country here was little known to Dirshan, for it was the region of the Bear and Wolf clans; but he did know that many bears had ranges that sometimes extended for twenty leagues. He would have thought her so weak from blood loss that she would not travel far, preferring to rest somewhere and gain strength. Yet that seemed not to be, for when the low sun reached midpoint, her trail led steadily onward, with Dirshan still following.

Then he found one reason for her haste. A narrow copse of wood fingered its way up a sheltered valley, the trail cutting diagonally across it and the stream below. Immediately on the other side was a small clearing and within, a ring of barren snow. Dirshan paused above it for a while; when nothing moved, he went in for a closer look.

The pack of wolves which he had heard before dawn had found the blood which they had smelled. Like him, they had followed to where it ended. Apparently the sow had chosen this clearing as a resting place; there was the beaten place under a bush where she had lain down. It was there they had come upon her. Four torn and ripped bodies of gray fur testified to the folly of their rush. Two of the carcasses had been ripped and torn by their pack mates, but the sow had not come off lightly. A widened and renewed blood trail now continued off up the steep slope of a rise. Dirshan rested for a while and had some of the dried meat before going on. From the quantity of blood which the bear was losing, she could not travel much farther; not, that was, unless she was the true god of the Bear clan. Dirshan did not think so.

Either his assessment of the sow's weakness was correct or she had finally reached the place for which she had been seeking when he finally came upon her. The trail angled upward through another belt of trees and then down into a narrow trough which sliced up into the mountains above. The snow was deeper here. Now cautious, Dirshan stepped lightly in the late-afternoon light, his footfalls making a small crunching noise in the snow crust. The trough became narrower, the tops of the ravine arcing up to almost meet above and block out what light was available. Here and there a tree grew, with a straight trunk that rose sheer beside the clifflike side to pierce the sky seeking for light and air. Suddenly the ravine opened out into a clearing, though the walls did not lose their steepness. Two groups of tall trees framed what appeared to be a narrow cave opening in the wall of rock that ended the ravine, the mouth a dark pit where no light penetrated.

Dirshan did not need the light nor the clear trail which led directly within to know this is where she would be. Bear stench was close in the air, as was the smell of something else long dead that was piled on a rock to one side of the entrance beneath the trees. No movement came from the opening, but Dirshan could hear a muted rumbling. The sow's breath, magnified perhaps by her cave? He did not know.

He slipped backward into the ravine and around a corner, disposing of all his extra gear. His left side was still stiff, each movement sending a lancing pain along his shoulder. He swung his arms to gain movement, but even as he tried to pull the heavy bow, he knew it would be impossible. Even should he succeed in pulling it back, his arm was so shaky that he would not be able to aim. It would have to be ax and knife.

As limber as possible, Dirshan looped the thong on the handle of the ax over his right wrist and searched for several rocks under the snow of the wall. Several likely ones came readily to hand, about the size of his fist. Then, taking one swift breath that exploded into his war cry as he came around the bend, he rushed into the clearing. The walls echoed and funneled his challenge into the dark opening as he stood in the center of the cleared space, feet wide apart and legs flexed. He counted on one stroke, but he wanted it to be final.

The sow's answer was not long in coming from the space before him; deep growls and roars roiled out of the darkness. But still the sow did not come out of her den; she waited on ground of her own choosing.

Dirshan was not fool enough to enter those cramped and dark quarters. Taking up one of the stones, he hurled it into the opening, hearing it strike a rock wall to clatter as it rolled.

"Hie Bear! Hie Bear!" he screamed as he hurled the next one, this time hearing it strike soddenly against something that grunted. The third stone brought the rush he wanted. With a powerful roar that belied her wounds, the sow came from the cave and charged.

But this was not the same bear. She was neither in the prime of her strength nor had she the fury of the night before. As she came into the light, Dirshan could see where she had been badly wounded, and there was a new raking cut along one side that exposed ribs. Apparently the wolves had had at least one good strike. And she limped, favoring that side with a loping stride that covered ground but was not the powerful rush of yesterday. For an instant, Dirshan almost pitied her, charging in her pride and pain to avenge her coming death: Just then a twinge in his neck warned him of his danger. His brother had died in those jaws, and there had been others.

Still, the sow moved incredibly fast, covering the three rods which separated them with great speed, even if she was clumsy. This time, weakened as she was by wounds and loss of blood, she did not rise on her haunches to embrace him; instead it was a simple charge to knock him over. Dirshan waited until the last moment before moving, her breath again acrid in his face, before he shifted his weight to one side and moved to the left. The tiny ax glittered and sang in the sun as it rose and fell once, the shock of the contact a muted chunk! in the windless air.

In that instant of contact, the sow's paw shot out, its claws raking deep furrows in Dirshan's leg as she shot past. He spun away, the force of the blow staggering him as his leg was opened up. The sow lumbered on for some steps before falling forward, almost skidding to a halt five feet from the opposite wall of the ravine. There was a final howl that died to a whimper of pain and was finally silent. The sow was dead, her spine cloven in twain by the spinning ax in Dirshan's hand. Her last blow had been reflex.

Yet it had done Dirshan great damage. Waves of dizziness gusted through his head as he dragged himself to one wall and used it to prop himself up. Red, raw meat stared open at him from his thigh and calf, though when he put his weight upon it, the kneecap did not give. The leg was still sound. Ignoring the waves of nausea which almost threatened to knock him over, he worked swiftly to rip up one of the spare shirts he had used as a makeshift sling and bound it tightly around his leg. A stick picked up from the litter around the cave mouth served as a brace to stiffen it. Then, ax still in his hand, he went over to look at his kill.

The ax had caught the bear directly behind the skull, severing her neck. This was the immediate cause of death, though Dirshan could now see that she would not have lived through the long winter. Somehow she had pulled out the arrow which had pierced her chest, but the gaping wound of its entrance still leaked red, as did the wound on her shoulder and the one behind the front paw. Dirshan looked at his brother's killer for some moments, sending silent thanks to Rema for victory. Though he would still have to get out of the highlands, a prospect which the weakened state of his body did not assure, he had done what he set out to do. But weakness was already making him stumble.

Knowing that to stop to rest now would be to invite stiffness and possible death should the cub return to this winter den, Dirshan forced himself to keep moving. A hastily gathered pile of dead wood served as the basis for a fire in front of the cave, which he did not want to enter because of the stench. His improvised shelter went up swiftly, and as it warmed itself and his scanty supply of clothes retrieved from around the bend in the trail, he went back to the carcass of the sow. Though numbed with cold and fatigue, he partially butchered it, taking care to remove all the claws—which would go to his brother's sons as a death trophy—and completely sever the head. This would come out with him from the highlands to prove the death of this clan totem. Last he carved out a couple of the flank steaks and propped them in front of the fire to grill while he tended his wounds.

The steaks sizzled and popped as their juices hit the fire

below while Dirshan unwrapped his leg. Though not surface wounds, none of the cuts was too serious; but what he really feared was corruption. For some reason no one knew, the claws of a bear carried some poison which immediately corrupted any cuts they made. Within days, healthy flesh turned purple and black and drained constantly. Dirshan took out his blade and laid it carefully on the coals before him. One final gulp from the gourd of fiery brandy which was in his pack, and he set to work. Sisss! and the first one was cauterized. Then, as he fought from fainting, he treated the others on his leg. For those in his neck and shoulder he could do nothing. They were in a bad location, and he knew he could not stand the pain of burning there. He would have to take his chances.

The three steaks, hot and half-raw, were rapidly gulped down, Dirshan ignoring the sweet taste of the bear meat as he gorged himself. Then he piled up the brush and lay down in front of the fire, pain and exhaustion almost making him faint. He knew he could do nothing if another bear were to come up to him, but with no sleep, he would simply faint and then indeed be easy prey for anything that chose to attack.

A sudden glancing slam on his back jerked him awake, the pain of his wounds forgotten as he scrambled to his feet. The flapping retreat of a mountain raven greeted his questing eyes, the new dawn above a flush which glinted on the blue-black feathers. Its comrades did not even flinch from their perch on the broad back of the carcass across from him as they picked and tore at the exposed flesh. Apparently the one which had landed on him thought him fair prey. Dirshan was grateful for its arrival. Had it not done so, he might have slept all day.

Stiff and sore were Dirshan's limbs, and his forehead was dry to the back of his hand. But he was moving, and that was what counted. He paced over to the carcass and removed several more steaks, building up the fire to grill them for breakfast. The flapping ravens did not retreat far, returning as soon as he left the mound of headless flesh. Such a feast in the highlands did not come often, and then was usually shared with the wolves.

As he ambled slowly around the clearing to get brush and wood for the fire—he had decided to stay in the ravine for another day of rest—Dirshan passed the dried carcass he had noted the day before. This time he took a closer look at it. What he saw made his hair rise—a superstition from his past to haunt him. The rack of tattered bones was not the carcass of some animal, dragged here by a carnivore. It was human. A female, moreover. But what really intrigued him was that it was stretched across a pile of carefully laid rocks. At each of the four endings of the scattered limbs were thongs of stretched leather. The woman, whoever she had been, had been staked out as sacrifice.

Dirshan looked upward from the pile of bones to the side of the cavern mouth, noting for the first time that there were faint, crude runes which had been incised into the rock, going up and over the irregular arch as far as a tall man could reach. Even more could be seen etched into the walls of what he had assumed to be only a bear's winter den. Dirshan's curiosity was aroused, though a shiver of anticipated danger went through his mind. He went back to the fire and retrieved his ax, then took up a burning faggot from the fire to serve as a torch. He would pass into the bear's den and find out why someone would take the time to stake out a woman before it.

Poking the torch before him to illuminate the blackness of the cave, he passed within, the stench from the bear a rising cloud before him.

III

The opening to what Dirshan had at first assumed was a natural cave was wide, well able to pass two men of his size as well as the dead sow bear. It cut straight into darkness for some distance, the weak light from Dirshan's improvised torch barely illuminating the vaulting ceiling. Yet even in that light he was able to see that the runes continued within, here deeply incised where the weather could not reach them. Here and there patches of color seemed to have been added for effect. Dirshan could not read the message in that script, for it was in a form and style which he had not learned; but he thought he recognized certain of the letters (if that was in fact what they were) as akin to old characters he had seen in the scriptorium in the archives of Alithar. Somehow he had the feeling that he did not wish to know what message they did convey, for he had the distinct impression that he was trespassing on forbidden ground. In his time in the Worlde, Dirshan had passed through many ancient places; places whose strange and evil holiness held meaning not only for the worshipers, but also danger for those who did not belong. Dirshan held no real belief in any gods—he had seen many die beneath his hand—but he did know that things had passed from the Worlde which should not be disturbed or bothered in these later times.

As he penetrated deeper into the cave, the mass of runes began to disappear, leaving only one line of cursive script that continued with him along the wall at shoulder height. A wide bend in the passage led off to the right and echoing darkness. The stench from the bear became an overpowering odor; the fetid, unmistakable blend of ripe and dead flesh mixed with the body smell of the sow. Now that the bend in the cave took him from the direct path of the entrance—the rock he hit the sow with must have bounced from the wall—and out of the wind-blown path of snow the floor was dry. At some places he could see paw prints where several bears had come and gone over the years. Suddenly his torch showed him a wider spot, a niche in the rock of the passage itself. Here the stench was heavy. There were splashes of dried blood high up on the walls and a pool, not quite crusted over, told of where she had lain the night before. Dirshan spat in the pool of blood to show his contempt and walked on. No bear would sleep there this winter, unless it was the yearling cub which he now knew the sow had chased off.

Once past that spot, the smell dissipated, but Dirshan went on, led by his curiosity and the line of continuing script. He followed it for some time before a burning sensation in his hand warned him that his torch would not last much longer. He hurriedly traced his path back to the entrance. Dirshan had no desire to be trapped deep in a cave, just as he was determined to find out what path was marked by the script.

He paused outside long enough to eat what remained of the bear steaks and drank some melted snow for water. Heaping more logs and brush on the fire, for it was already beginning to snow again and he did not relish the thought of restarting the fire on his return, he took up several of the smaller faggots, and, with one already lit, retraced the mystery path.

This time Dirshan counted his steps, and after some four hundred-odd, came to the first branch in the tunnel. By this time the cold in the cave had taken on a uniform temperature, and here and there the glint of ice that sheeted over some small break in the rock walls threw reflections back at him as he passed. Still the guiding script led onward, forking to the right as he followed it. Several more turns were taken, and then the passage he was using suddenly opened up into a rocky grotto too large for his feeble light source to illuminate. He stood on the threshold and wondered what to do next.

His shout reverberated and returned many echoes as he tried

to judge the space in the cavern. It was huge, as he could already judge because of the large girth and size of the pillars which rose from floor to unseen ceiling to support the beginnings of the roof. He walked outward to the closest of these, its slick ribbed sides throwing back a white and translucent reflection of his face. Dirshan had seen such caves before. There were many such in the neighborhood of Anshan many leagues to the west. He knew they were natural, but never had he seen any with writing on their walls.

Returning to his entrance into the cavern, he debated the wisdom of going on, even though the written path was plain to his right. His curiosity left him no choice. Lighting a fresh torch from his dwindling supply, he went on. Anyone who had taken such pains to carve the script must have had something at the end of it.

The writing worked its way around the circumference of the cavern. Over a thousand steps were passed in this before the script turned another corner and entered another tunnel. This new passage was much narrower, and there was a strong draught of cold air that blew into his face. In the light of the guttering torch, Dirshan carefully picked his way, his interest dimming as each step seemed to get colder and colder. Then he gradually began to notice a change in the character of the walls; whereas heretofore they had been solid rock, now they began to be coated with ice, thin at the start and then thicker as he passed on. Even the floor began to take on this glazed texture, the surface slippery under the thick soles of his boots. Once he lost his footing, to come down with a hard thump that sent shards of pain up his injured leg. After that he became careful, watching not only where he put his feet but also consciously watching for handholds along the smooth walls. He would not have gone on had not the writing still beckoned him from underneath the coating of ice. There was a sudden turn in the tunnel where it seemed to almost bend back on itself. It was as he groped his way carefully around it that the accident happened.

Only it was no accident. The glassy surface under his feet

seemed to give way beneath him, his mind saying, "Why, it's pivoted!" just as he was tipped forward to slide down, the torch flying from his hand. In that brief flare of light as the lit torch arced in the air, Dirshan saw a long, sloping decline in the tunnel before and below him, paved with ice that led almost directly downward. The jar of his fall knocked the breath from his lungs. Yet he had the presence of mind to drop the bundle of faggots under his arm and grip the haft of the ax he still carried. It was a bumping and sliding trip down that slope; he caromed off at least two walls before his good leg kicked him into the center to slide smoothly downward for some distance. He came to rest with a jarring thud in utter darkness.

Lying there, afraid to move for fear that he had not gone the full distance down that natural slide, his first impression was of absolute cold. While fresh, the bite of the air was bitter, its smell telling of dead cold and frozen things that did not stir in the hot summer. Once his breath returned, he cautiously began to feel around himself, attempting to find out where he was in the pitch-black darkness. He had a great fear that there would be a further slope to the road on which he had just fallen.

But the area around him was smooth and level, though ice covered. He carefully braced himself with the haft of the ax and levered himself erect. Nothing seemed broken, though his back felt as if he had been repeatedly buffeted by the dead bear. Inching himself around, he first discovered that he was surrounded by ice-covered walls, and then the beginning of the slope down which he had passed. Now that he had a chance to think, he realized that he had been thrown; the whole floor had pivoted under him. It must have been some type of counter-weighted deadfall, though knowing about it would not help him now. Dropping back to his hands and knees, he felt around the bottom of the slope, his reward the dry bark of one of the faggots which had come down the slope with him. He muttered a few thanks to Rema for having had the foresight to include his tinder and flint when he embarked on this journey as he lit the torch. It was a time-consuming process which the constant wind from his back did nothing to help, but he finally succeeded.

When he turned to survey his surroundings by its light, he almost wished he had not bothered.

What came to Dirshan's eyes in a glittering multifaceted reflection was a death house. A long chamber, square cut, led off into dimness, sheathed with the rime of centuries. Spaced along the walls which seemed to pierce the heart of the mountain were niches and in each niche was a corpse. Dirshan was familiar with the dead; he had sent many beyond the Veil with his own hand; but even in the newly dead there was a quality of absence, the feeling that whoever had owned that body was now gone. Not so with these remnants of the dead past. Each of them had a brooding air of alertness, the effect heightened by the fact that all their eyes were open and glittered in the light of the torch.

Muttering an oath, Dirshan nerved himself to pass closer to the nearest of these undead, discovering, as he came closer, that it was covered with a coating of ice. Several seemed to grin at him, and there was one which must have died by violence, judging by the cloven skull and smashed eye. All were alike in dress: a sort of leather robe that was drawn around the bodies and clan markings were blue whorls and lines that stitched paths across their faces. Dirshan passed down the line of bodies, noting that all had the same type of facial markings and dress, though several had a different type of jewelry. Each corpse sat in a humped pose, the hands carefully gripping a short sword as it rested stiffly under the ice.

There was no sense of decay under the never-changing ice, and Dirshan had no way of discovering what or how long these bodies had lain here, protected by cold and the spirits of their ancestors. Yet the line on both sides was long, with a corpse at regular intervals of perhaps five steps. Dirshan was able to note that some seemed to come from more recent times, for at least once he recognized a set of dangling beads as having come from Anshan in the west. There were several empty niches toward the end of the line. Then the cave branched off to one side into a carven hollow thrice as large as all the rest. This was the resting place of the largest man Dirshan had ever seen, living or dead—a true king of the dead.

Judging solely by the thickness of ice which covered the massive corpse on its throne, Dirshan thought that it may have lain here for at least one Great Cycle of the Worlde, if not longer. Fully ten inches of clear ice separated his face from the brooding form of the silent figure on a throne, who seemed to sit in malice waiting for a resurrection that would never come. A king he would have had to have been, for when living he would have topped Dirshan's height by at least a foot. Red glaring eyes stared out of a forehead marked by the blue whorls, the head topped by white hair. There were no lines graven in the face, but Dirshan had an impression of age-old evil. A simple tunic of silver graced the form, in the center of which hung an intricate torque from a golden chain. Around the corpse were the accouterments of a war chief and leader; two slaves with split skulls rested silently beneath their leader, each of his feet planted on a head as mute testimony to his power when alive. Dirshan gazed for some moments at this figure, drawn by the feeling of power that seemed to emanate from it. He wondered what manner of man he had been in the days of his youth, and what resulted from his rule? It was a fruitless question—this corpse would not answer. As he went to turn away, Dirshan was attracted by the glitter that flared and danced from the torque hung over the chest. Dirshan fought for a moment with himself, superstition of dishonor to the dead warring with his knowledge that the dead had no need for such trifles as weapons or jewels. Finally he commended the man's soul to Rema and with a shattering crash that echoed in the long tunnel, began to hack at the ice. It crashed and tinkled as it fell to the floor under his blows.

Dirshan's fingers were almost as frozen as the corpse's as he groped and tore to remove the torque. Luckily the clasp had slipped down around the neck and he was finally able to pull it free. Examined in the torchlight, it was a curious thing; a metal seeming to be a mixture of gold and silver with runes graven over the heavy surface. A sudden guttering from the torch told Dirshan that he would do better to spend his time getting away from the cave, and so, after saluting the corpse with the ax, he tucked the torque into his pouch and turned away. The body merely grinned at him evilly; his last impression was that a red eye seemed to wink with glee. Dirshan shook off the feeling of awe and passed onward.

After the dead king, there were no more niches. The cave suddenly narrowed into a tunnel as the ice walls seemed to crowd together, the wind issued from the unseen end coming with increased force. The torch flared to warn Dirshan, and he expected the dead end to which he came.

He had already assumed that there would be no back entrance, for otherwise those who had spent much time in building it would not have bothered to put such a trap in the front door. He hurried back to the point where the slope ended in this underground world, picking up another of the faggots and lighting a new torch. He stood on the slope and looked upward, holding the torch high. Far above in the glittering mirage of repeated reflections, he could make out the turn where the tunnel began—perhaps thirty paces. Knowing that it would be futile, he still attempted to climb it, falling backward after only three steps on the slick surface. There he stopped to think of a way out of his dilemma.

Several times in his youth, Dirshan's father had taken him up to the great glacier, which, like a frozen cliff that glittered and sparkled in the sun, could be seen far above the great valley of smoking water that was the center of his homeland. The stream which issued from it was the start of the great river; it was a test of manhood to swim its rushing turbulence at the point where it came out from the ice wall. When climbing, his father had given him steel points that strapped to the feet, and even with those there was need for an ice ax to dig into the glaring surface. Dirshan had no such tools, but he did now have both an ax and his knife. His mind told him that those who had placed the bodies here had to have a means of getting out. He began to carefully examine the floor of the slide under the ice, paying attention to where the walls met the floor.

His interest was rewarded when he saw under the layer of ice a series of slots carved into the walls. They were spaced about a foot and a half up each wall on both sides, chisel marks evident under the coating of rime. Apparently whoever brought down the bodies for burial first slid down a number of logs cut to fit across the icy width of the slope. The ice would then be cut away at each side by the slots and a log wedged across to serve as a step, a ladder built from the bottom up. Dirshan did not know how they passed the pivoted section above, but he would see when he got that far. Of course once the body was placed, the burial party would retreat upward, pulling up a log at a time as they went. Water coursing down the slope would seal off the slots again. It was clever—Dirshan could well appreciate it; though he thought he would appreciate it even more if he was not caught at the bottom. Traps look much better from the outside than from within.

In any case, he could not use their method; he did not have the materials. Left with no choice but brute force in the numbing cold, he prepared for the ascent. He would need a hand on both ax and knife; yet there would be a need for light as he inched his way upward. The only alternative was his teeth. Spread-eagling himself on the slope, he wedged the piny butt of the torch in his mouth; one hand gripping the haft of the ax, the other the knife. And thus, inch by bitter inch, he crawled his way out of the ice-rimed hole in the mountain.

The constant wind from behind him blew the acrid smoke of the torch which rested on his shoulder into his face, almost blinding him. His upward journey was a constant series of chopping so that he could get a bite with the blade of the ax, pulling himself level with it, and then anchoring his place with the driven point of the knife. A third of the way upward, an attack of coughing almost caused him to lose his hard-won ground; he clung to the hilt of Akamatoth, which anchored him in place while his ax hand held the torch away from his seared nostrils. Done, he continued upward, every foot gained a constant pull and ripping on his injured shoulder. But he persisted, the corpses in their icy rest below him a reminder of what would happen if he failed.

He was almost to the point where the tunnel took its sudden sharp bend when he came to the pivoted section. Balanced as he was, he could not rise to see the full extent of the tilting slab, but the slightest pressure of his hand was enough to tilt it downward toward him. Those who built it had contrived cunningly, for Dirshan could see that the entire width of the floor tilted forward. It was not a section which could be jumped or bypassed. There he rested for a moment, trying to think of a way to get past into the natural cave which beckoned a scant ten feet away.

Dirshan carefully examined the leading edge of the slab, finding that it was carved to slide smoothly on the rock and ice adjoining it. The slightest pressure made it tilt forward, then return level with the floor.

Only one idea suggested itself. Groping in his pouch, he removed some of the golden coins currently used in the Empire; the incised city of the straits showing its proud towers to his eyes. For a brief moment, he wished he was now taking his ease in one of them; then he remembered that this journey was his own choice. Using the edge of the ax, he scored a groove in the ice-covered joint between the block of stone and the solid floor, shaving away the ice to the bare stone. When the groove was deep enough, he placed the coins edgewise in the slot as far as they would go, using the flat of the ax as a hammer, the gold in its softness flattening out under the pounding. Once the improvised wedges were in place, Dirshan then pressed on the leading edge of the pivoted section. It made noise, but the wedges seemed to hold.

Dirshan crawled forward carefully, inching his way upward onto the slab, its constant trembling beneath him a warning that it might not hold. His full length was finally upon it. Stretching forward with the ax unbalanced him. The slab began to tilt. Disregarding caution, Dirshan levered himself forward on the point of the knife, the ax biting deep as he brought it down past the forward edge of the slab. One lurching scramble and he was up and over the tilting block, only his feet full upon it. There he lay for some time after taking the torch from his mouth, his breath short and cheek cold on the floor.

Again it was the torch which warned him that he would not have time to rest in these surroundings. A few feet forward and he was beyond the slope, finally able to stand erect. Leaning against the wall, he raised the torch high, gazing down at the long slope which had almost claimed him.

Yes, the builders had made it well. Their dead would sleep in their cold rest with little or no disturbance from man or beast. Dirshan wondered briefly what god or gods those men below had worshiped, and then dismissed it. He did not really care, and the dead no longer have a need for questions. But as he turned to leave this strange place, his thought went back to those red eyes glaring below in the darkness which reigned there. What had they seen in the cycles that had passed and would continue to pass while their owner waited for his release?

His path out was swift, for he did not tarry as he left the cave system. He made it to the cavern and the end of the ice walls before his torch finally snuffed itself out in a cloud of piny smoke. But by then he knew where he walked and had only to guide himself with his left hand riding on the band of script beneath it. By the time he reached the section where the bear had made its den, fresh and chill air warned him of the coming entrance. He had made it.

It was full dark by the time he reached the entrance, and his fire had died down to embers, casting just enough light to show him the flitting forms of scavengers as they worried the carcass across the clearing. Dirshan piled on more wood and basked in the roaring flame, thankful that some warmth came into his flesh after the frozen deeps behind and below him. A burning sensation on one cheek—the one which had lain on the ice-covered floor as he ascended, told him that he had been frostbitten there; but a small injury was a cheap price to pay for the chance to escape death. He watched as two more steaks grilled on a couple of sticks. He wanted to examine the torque, but decided to wait for daylight. Even when he put his hand close to it in the pouch, it had a disturbing chill which contact with his body did not seem to dispel. But for now he was content to be alive and watch the scavengers as they ripped and tore at the meat beyond the firelight.

IV

Toward the end of the night it started to snow again, this time more heavily. Wanting to avoid being buried under the same kind of drift that was making a vague mound of snow out of the half-chewed bear carcass, Dirshan finally decided that the stench immediately inside the cave was not *that* bad. He moved those of his possessions as he could find inside the mouth out of the wind, building up a new fire, and finally bedded down for the night. He could not fight snow.

He woke to a world of glittering whiteness, though the clouds had rolled away to dump their heavy load on farther slopes. A brilliant sun pricked icy points of sharp light out of the heaped drifts, some bushes almost buried under their coating. Dirshan walked out into the narrowest part of the cleft, there to find that the wind had piled it up almost to his waist. It would be a sore trip out, especially as he would be burdened with wounds and the trophies of his hunt. But he knew these mountains; root and branch, peak and vale. In this season, almost any letup of the outpouring of snow was an opportunity to move. He would take it.

His wounds were stiff, especially the ones in his neck, and the muscle aches which answered his movements told him of his own condition. Yet experience also told him that it was exercise which would cure much of it; that is, if he did not tarry to let his body become stiff. After one last meal taken on the bear's flesh around the warming fire, he began to pack his goods for a return both to Gett and the base camp. As he carefully fingered and then packed away the stripped head and claws of his brother's killer, his teeth bared in a grimace, remembering both the fight and his close brush with death. The torque which he had removed from the icy corpse beneath the mountain he also stowed away in the pouch—not because he did not want to wear it, but it would not seem to warm, even when placed close to the fire. A necklace of piercing-cold metal was not an ornament for winter. He put off consideration of this strange effect until he was out of the highlands.

Finally, he strapped on the improvised snowshoes which would distribute his weight and prevent his sinking into the crusted snow. Soot from the burnt end of a stick was rubbed under his eyes. Dirshan had once seen a man who had become snow-blind, and he had no desire to wander into some crevasse because of it. Before the sun reached the top of its arc, he was on his way. The shallow depressions left by his plodding feet left no mark after some seconds under the wind, rapidly wiped out by windblown snow. No trace would remain of his passage, a trespasser in the world of beasts without man.

It took Dirshan three days to reach the base camp that he and Gett had erected, although what seemed an age had passed. He anticipated only two days' travel, but for some reason the snow seemed to follow him down, even when he was below the line where snow did not usually fall in this season. For this reason he had to lay over two nights in natural windbreaks, arising each morn to a world of fresh whiteness and covered tracks. By the third day, he again entered regions more familiar to him, even after the passage of so many cycles, and here and there he came upon isolated steads; all, he was sad to note, seemed abandoned. Aliffa would feel the brunt of Dirshan's trek keenly once he was close enough to the man to do so; the point driven home would be of steel.

Gett was up and stirring in the fading light as Dirshan approached the base camp, but there was another, darker shape beside the fire. Dirshan had reacted with his usual caution on approaching the camp, coming in over a ridge line in heavy brush to view the scene before walking in. Though the other did not seem to pose much of a threat, especially judging by Gett's unconcern, he was still wary. He wasted a futile half-hour in the cold looking for some trace which would indicate others lying in wait. He found none. Dirshan finally approached cautiously through the trees, hoping to get within earshot of the fire. What he heard was not expected:

"Come on into the camp, Dirshan the God-killer," a low, melodious voice of indeterminate gender said in his native tongue. "The wind again begins its call and the fire is warm." Gett said nothing. He simply stared fixedly into the flames. Dirshan walked into his view, but the silent figure of his companion did not even glance at him in interest. Dirshan put hand to his sword, half-drawing it. His will felt strangely weak.

"What have you done to him?" Dirshan heard himself ask thickly. His tongue felt encased in a mouthful of honey.

"Ah!" said the figure, the face shrouded by a concealing cowl, the body seeming to shift in the dark robe. "Then the portents were right! No spell can fully hold you. Put up thy sword and put down your burden. Your companion here can neither see nor hear us. I have given him a dream of the distant Heclos. He now rides the waves, far from this snowy stand of trees." The voice was still hushed, but carried power.

Feeling the warmth of the fire and realizing that there was nothing he could really do unless he knew more, Dirshan did as the figure suggested and dumped his pack beside the construction of sticks and branches which served as a windbreak. He took a place beside the fire, midway between Gett and the now-silent figure. He examined the robe in silence as he held his hands to the flame, seeking some clue to its identity. But nothing was there besides a dark hole, behind which he assumed (and hoped) was a human face and hands concealed in the flowing robe which completely covered the whole figure.

"Hmmm!" the figure said, as if musing. "A man of some silence, and one who protects his own. Curious that even though you know nothing of this, nor what has happened to your man, that you should automatically place yourself in a position to defend him should need arise. And against that which you know nothing of!" There was a pause. "A man who is armored in faith, convinced of his own prowess, or perhaps just stupid?"

Again a pause.

"But no matter—time will tell as with all things. I have come a long distance to see thee. But I did not know until I came that it would be you! A man of courage and luck, a breaker of oaths and Empires, slayer of false gods! All these things, and yet a man, frail beaker to hold such hope. For you can die. And yet . . . yet . . ."

The monologue was broken by the harsh cadences of Dirshan's voice. "Cease this! I need no praise from nameless ones in the snow of my homeland. Tell me who you are and what you seek from me to follow so deeply into this wilderness."

"Ah, how often is haste the bane of the short-lived! But no board games—both of us have tasks to do. I am called Iyali, though I have had many names. Know you aught of it?"

Dirshan searched his mind and could find no memory. He said as much, adding, "What should it mean to me?"

"Nothing." The voice sighed. "I often do not realize how much time has passed through the Worlde since I was last about. Names are important, though, as you should know. They will often tell you more about a place or person than the actual presence itself, for they will tell you what people truly think of that object. I have come to you here for three reasons. You are involved in all three, though I had not known that it would be one so famous."

Dirshan made a sound of disgust and spat into the fire. "I need nothing of this mummery. Release my servant and be-gone. I have much to do on the morrow and need sleep." Yet his curiosity was aroused, though he kept it from his voice.

"You have not the taste for word games, but such is to be expected, since you sit here and not in the court at Alithar." Dirshan started despite his control, wondering how much Gett had revealed in his ignorance. He really wanted some time alone with him. "Do not be harsh in thought to your companion," Iyali said, seeming to echo Dirshan's very thoughts. "He has not spoken much to me except for your name, nor can I read his mind. The spell has been in effect for most of the time since I have entered this camp.

"The information which I have is freely available to any that can listen to the wind. It whispers much of the abilities and activities of Dirshan on behalf of the Empire. And I have many contacts, some of whom you have met in your travels.

"How I know is of no interest to you, since I already do. But you have returned. And that is of importance to me since you did so at this time and place. If you will not interrupt me with questions, I will explain.

"Roughly five cycles past, I was far to the north, at the time striving to pierce the darkness of the future to foretell what paths the Worlde would take before I journeyed out again upon it. I do not often do so in this later time. Yet in that forelooking I discovered that the future was shrouded; you would understand better if I said that there was as if a wall had been placed in my sight. The upcoming outline of the battle between League and Empire was fairly clear, as was the probable outcome. Indeed, even your then-future involvement in it was there for the sharp eye to see.

"Before you interrupt again, let me add that I could not see *you*—that is, Dirshan the individual. Reading the future is an exercise in perhaps, the lines converge at certain points, and if you know some of the lines from which they spring, you can see the whole pattern. One knows that water will turn to ice in winter, but what is that magic point at which it does? It is fairly simple to read what comes if one has the tools. It is not that a man will remake his own time, but time and place which give a man the opportunity to allow him to rise above his fellows—if that makes any sense."

The figure paused in silence, finally reaching out one shrouded hand—Dirshan preferred to think of it as such, though he could not see it—and picked up a stick to stir the fire. Sparks leaped up into blackness. "In any event, you happened to be there and took advantage of a situation as it was presented to you. That should have been the end of one crisis, and if things had worked out as they normally do, you would have taken over the throne of the Empire, in the process deposing the Family and ruling—"

"I sought not that," Dirshan broke in violently, stung by the comment.

The cowled head moved. "But you could have had it, and in your heart you know it to be true. New blood is needed in the Empire's ruling line; a fact which was recognized by the founder and why it has always accepted or promoted the competent in order to take them before it was overthrown. Though you are right in your unspoken knowledge that it would have been the death of you, Dirshan the man, even as it revitalized what was becoming moribund and static. That may still be your fate, though I cannot see it. On the other hand, that may have been only a preparation for what is to come. And that is why I am here at this time and place.

"I will digress for some time to speak of history, of the time before your people came to occupy this land. Before they came into possession, others lived here. That was a cold and austere people, from out of the far east. Over two Great Cycles of the Worlde have passed since they ruled—time for Empires to rise and topple in ashes—and they were never conquered nor driven off. They held to nothing but their own beliefs and rituals. Except for the constant raiding which made them the bane of near and far neighbors in order to satisfy their particular needs, they were content. Many tried to subdue them; all failed."

"That is not true," Dirshan said. "I know the history of my own people, for the Rememberers still hold to this knowledge of far times. This land was empty when we came to it."

"Yes, it was. But that was because they had decided to withdraw and leave for another, farther into the east. Their quasi-immortal king who had led them was finally destroyed, and the following line of lesser men could not hold together what he had created, though they tried. I suspect that another reason was that under the effects of their constant raiding, other peoples and tribes withdrew under the pressure, making it ever more difficult to supply their needs. They were—and are—flesh-eaters—the flesh of men. With the destruction of Cleyungit, the power was gone.

"I can see that the question has occurred to you: What has

this to do with me and mine? But it is very close to you, the
source of many of your coming troubles.

"This people, who are now called the Ayal, retreated east in
order to protect their beliefs and source of food; for they devel-
oped a breeding stock of humans to supply their tables. Unlike
cattle, men will escape; so they settled them on a large mountain island in the center of the Black Meer, far in the east,
knowing that they could not thus easily escape the knife."

Dirshan spat noisily into the fire, disgust plain on his face. It
was known that flesh-eaters lived east of the mountains, but
there was many a trackless league between them and Dirshan's
tribe. Gett said nothing, still wrapped in his dream.

"Yes," the voice said, "I see you hold to the feelings of your
own people and those of the west. Yet it is possible that you
would think differently had you been born to this belief."

"Why was not such filth driven from the Worlde? Breeding
men to eat! It would call for a purge!"

"In earlier cycles, men also held to your feelings; but there
was a lack of power to resist them, and once they had passed
away from sight and sound . . . men simply gave thanks for another scourge departed from their Worlde. With Cleyungit
broken, they had to retreat, out of the sight of men who could
no longer be kept at bay. There, in the center of a huge lake of
great bitterness called the Black Meer, is the mountain island
called Timgimial. On the banks of that meer they constructed
a city, called Cascalon; their breeding stock confined to the island. There they have stayed for at least one Great Cycle."

"And you now seek someone to root them out? This is not a
task for one man, nay, even for the whole Order! I am not at-
tached to any of the Chapters, and they would not follow my
lead. If so many leagues lay between them and us, it would
seem to be of import only for conversation, not action."

"Be not so sure that the Order as a whole would not follow
your lead, Dirshan, should you chose to exercise the authority
which your power has earned you. But no matter how you consider it, you will come into contact with the Ayal. For even
now some of them are on the march—and they march west.

One of the things I heard most clearly was the screams of those they caught on the way, and that was a future which happens now."

"So, you came to give me warning. If true, I am in some debt; though I do not see what good it is to know of a disaster if known beforehand. Yet I have another task already before me; and these Ayal, as you call them, are still far away." He did not mention what Ke'in had said to him in Alithar before departing. "There is widespread disruption here in the clans, a wound which has to be healed even before any thought can be given to an outside assault."

"I agree. But it is plain that one of my tasks was to give you this warning, for this doom will shortly fall on this land, and someone should know of the extent of the danger. They will not be turned away by the thought of fighting; even as they fall, the dead will go to feed the living."

Dirshan sat in thought for a moment. "There would seem to be nothing here for them to attack; all this land produces is danger and mouths in abundance. Surely these carrion will not fight simply for an old homeland? No one here would relinquish it without causing them much loss."

"They have several reasons. Before the war arose between League and Empire, the Order was on the offensive and had begun to press upon their borders to the west. In doing so, it has destroyed the isolation which the Ayal sought and which up to that time they had successfully kept about them. You are aware, of course, what the reaction of the Order would be once they discovered those particular beliefs the Ayal hold?"

"Instant death. None would be spared."

"Exactly, so in that sense the Ayal could only sit and await what would eventually come to them. Their reaction was to attack, boasted by a prophecy that they would someday come out and regain what they had once lost. They do not, of course, know exactly who or what opposes them. They were very isolated, there in the dark city by the Meer. Then the Worlde came back to them, bearing fire and sword.

"They also have another problem, which has only recently

come to my ears. Too many people. Because of their history of raiding, they have an overabundance of trained fighting men who were a constant problem at home and threatened to overturn the system as it stood. The obvious ploy was to turn these men outward; when the Order came onto the scene, things proceeded apace. Now they feel they march on natural enemies.

"As to why they will turn here first; well, all people have a past. Theirs was centered not far from here. That is what partially draws them." The voice was low and drawn.

Dirshan pursed his lips, cold biting the backs of his hands and making him shiver. "You know much of these matters for a stranger. Whence comes it?"

"I do not have to explain the source of these matters to you, nor my knowledge," the voice said menacingly, giving Dirshan the urge to unsheathe his weapon. "I said I foresaw some of this five cycles ago. I have not been idle since. This is not some small thing to concern merely the Garazi in their mountain home, even though it is a big interest of yours. It has taken some time to discover what I have told you in a short while. They come here mainly to regain the talisman that was carried by Cleyungit, which was put with him when he fell so many cycles ago. With the power so contained, they could go on to conquer the Worlde, if they have someone with the power and knowledge to wield them."

Dirshan's mind instantly leaped to the past and the icy burial chamber beneath the mountain. The fixed, staring eyes of the giant entombed there came immediately to his thought. "The ice cave!" he exclaimed. "That was his crypt!"

"Yes," his informant said. "That, too, was something I saw in the future before it closed down. You removed the torque, then? It was clear it was taken, but not by whom."

"Yes," Dirshan answered, his hand going immediately to his pouch and removing the fur-wrapped object. "But it will not warm, so I did not wear it as trophy." He held it up.

To Dirshan's eye, the figure seemed to flinch at the sight.

"It is always cold, like the power and force of its owner. That is its power. Have you not noticed that snow comes more frequently at night, though this is still the early part of the season? The torque draws it from the heights, as it also can draw the heat and power from those who oppose its wielder. As you go away from the mountains, its power will lessen, for it must have something to work with. One cannot make snow out of sand. But this is the main talisman which they seek, and they will not stop until they see it on the neck of he who leads them."

Dirshan made a gesture as if to throw it into the fire. "Then let us destroy this talisman, and they will seek it in vain."

The figure raised its arm, denial in the gesture. "That was the second of my reasons for coming here to speak with you. The first to warn of the Ayal; the second to say that you should not destroy the torque, if that should be in your power. You have the reputation of tossing away such powerful objects— even giving them away if you do not want them yourself. Who else is now abroad in the Worlde who would use a sacrificial blade—the one at your side—as a mere weapon? But this thing has now come to you, and I judge that you have the strength to wield it if necessary. I say keep the torque."

"Why should I not give it unto you? Apparently you know more of its uses. Use it yourself if it has power."

"I cannot. It must be held and directed by a male; it is keyed to those forces in the Worlde." Dirshan gave no outward sign, but the figure had just seemed to indicate that it was, in fact, a woman. Then, in an instant, it occurred to him that it could be of no sex at all—perhaps something else entirely. "If you will not wear it," she continued, "at least retain it. I see it as part of what you must do."

Dirshan shrugged and rewrapped it before putting it back into his pouch. He had no real use for such things, though in the past he had had occasion to come upon them. He felt all such should be cast into the fire; a man was what he was without such talisman's power. "What is the third reason for your presence here? More dark counsel?"

"You have paid attention. The first to warn, the second to speak of the torque. The third is more of a request. I wish to travel with you for some little time. Consider it a fair exchange for the information, if you will. I will not be a hindrance on your journey."

It was on Dirshan's lips to say he would not have a woman traveling with him, and then it again came to him that he did not know for sure that this was a woman. And had not it (she?) quieted Gett, who despite his small, sly appearance was not one to take lightly?

Dirshan tried a different tack. "I know not what my path will be for some time. It may mean I go into some danger, many times alone. Those of my companions who will face it with me . . . well . . . I would choose . . ."

"Those you already know and trust?" The statement was finished for him. "But in one sense you are always alone, even before the comfort of your own hearth. The reach of the Ayal stretches far, already your own land is in turmoil. I can be a valuable ally. Already I have traveled a great distance to speak with you. What I ask is a little thing."

"True," Dirshan admitted. But he still wanted no companion whose motives he did not know. He switched subjects. "You said my land is in turmoil. Though it was told me that Aliffa has allied himself with the eaters-of-the-dead . . . still, he is of the Garazi. All would leave him—nay, kill him on the suspicion—rather than mix their forces into conquering their own land. Rebel against the Order? Aye, in a sense even I have done that. But to wield blade beside flesh-eaters? No, not even the man who killed my father."

"One does not assume that the sword knows how or why it is being used, for death is a natural function which requires no question on its part; and even if it should speak and question, would it know that the hand that uses it intended to toss it into the fire afterward? I think not. Aliffa did not seek this ally, nor does he know the extent to which he may be used. But I have the knowledge of my own inquiries. While the Order has turned to fight this small battle at its rear, the Ayal advance without let or hindrance. The exact way in which this was done is not clear, but the results are plain before us. Perhaps this could be the lever by which to stop him—I do not know. But he serves their purpose."

Dirshan suddenly caught himself whistling a short snatch of tune, popular in Alithar and based on a marching song of the Order called "Advance to Glory." It made his decision. "You may travel with me, and I will give what protection I can. But it appears"—he glanced significantly at Gett—"that I cannot offer much help in the face of your own powers."

"The dream." And here Iyali laughed, a mirthful sound that seemed out of place in the darkness. "It takes more than you think to produce such an effect; it is not like snapping a finger under one's nose. As using a sword will tire you, doing this tires me. Even as I speak, I must concentrate to keep him in his dream. His will is very strong."

"Aye, then release him. But before, I have one question. Why is it you interest yourself in this matter? The affairs of the Ayal or the Garazi—even the Order—would seem to be apart from your interest." He looked inquiringly at the form.

There was a sigh, one could call it of great weariness, and then an answer which Dirshan would think about for some time. "It concerns me greatly, more than I can speak of. But having once taken up a task, it cannot lightly be put down again. It was I who placed Cleyungit under the guise that holds him to the ice cave. I would not see him loose in the Worlde again."

Dirshan did not inquire further; he already had much to ponder. "How is it we will explain your presence to Gett? He will have some questions."

"My presence to him will be as natural as if I walked into this camp with you earlier. Indeed, that is how it shall be." There was a very faint, but audible snap! which sounded like a bowstring breaking. Gett stirred, moving as if from a dream.

"Ah, Dirshan," he said on looking up and seeing Dirshan. "There is something about this snow which makes one dream of the warmth and wetness of the Heclos. Would you and our guest have some soup? A couple of careless rabbits have been cooking all afternoon, and I, for one, am eager to try them."

Dirshan looked at him for a moment, and then back to the shrouded form. "Yes," he finally replied. "And then to bed. Both of us have traveled far today, and I want an early start in the morn." He piled more wood on the fire and sat in silence, thinking, while Gett served the food. Despite the warmth, Dirshan did not find it easy to sleep that night.

V

All were awake with the dawn, the first pale light coming over the serried hills behind them and illuminating a world that had received another cover of white during the night. Despite his exertions and great fatigue, Dirshan had not gotten much sleep. Much of his night had been spent tossing on his narrow couch of furs, mulling over the information which Iyali had given him. His brain was filled with questions, the most pressing being the shape and character of his new traveling companion. His thoughts on the matter had not produced any answers. And he was half-afraid to ask the questions aloud.

Iyali—man, woman, beast, even it? That was his first question; at any rate, a creature which did not seem to sleep. Each time Dirshan had rolled over and peered past the swirl of snow out toward the fire, that figure was sitting in the same spot, occasionally poking the fire with a stick. Dirshan had speculated on what manner of creature did not need sleep or protection from the cold. He did not like where those speculations led him. There was something in the silent figure of death, that silent watcher who merely waits for what it knows will sooner or later occur so that it can convey one beyond the Veil and into the presence of Rema. Dirshan wished he had some kind of positive faith to sustain him in his doubt and provide some answers. All he had was this darkling figure beside the fire, backdropped by little eddies of snow. There was a small voice also in the back of his mind that he would do better to put an arrow into the figure; but even though his instincts prevented it, he had the feeling that it would not work.

As usual, Gett had fallen into a stupor as soon as he lay

down; snoring mightily for some time until Dirshan kicked
him to make him roll over. Then it was suddenly morn and his
turn to dodge a foot—this time from Gett. It had greatly disturbed the other servants in the Pillars at Alithar that Gett
used such insulting familiarity with Dirshan. Once he had permitted the little man to administer a lesson in civility to one of
them. He valued Gett for his abilities, of which he knew the
limits, and not for what other people thought of him.

"Dirshan," his voice had added. "Time to rise. Our guest
and I have been up for a hand's passage of the sun. Food is
prepared."

Dirshan said nothing; only risen, as those whom sleep have
not comforted, and went out to squat beside the fire, the chill
light of the new morn only making the rising worse. He had decided before finally falling asleep that with some reservations,
he would take Iyali's words as truth. As Gett busied himself un-
covering the narrow latrine that had been dug away from the
main campsite, Dirshan said to the hooded figure, "I have
given much thought to your words of last night. Only one
thing has bothered me. Are you man or woman? Or does that
robe hide the form of a beast?"

The hole in the hood turned to face him. The light of morn
did not pierce its darkness, which seemed to brood in quiet
questioning. "I am no beast," the voice said, for some reason
higher and more resonant than the night before, "though I can
appear as that to some eyes. What would you have?"

"It seems to me that while perhaps Gett will not question
your presence, there will be others and many of them. I know
not your powers, but apparently you could not control both
Gett and myself, for otherwise you would have done so last
night. Therefore . . ." It was an unstated question.

"A good point," the voice mused. "And my powers of illu-
sion in that respect are not unlimited. Therefore to the Worlde
I will appear as I am. . . ." And a hand came out of the en-
veloping sleeve and pulled back the cowl, exposing the face.

Dirshan was quite prepared for a shock, but the face which
revealed itself was quite ordinary—at least to outward show. It

was female, with long brown hair that disappeared under the dropped hood. Two brilliant blue eyes shone from under a deep brow; the nose snubbed, the mouth generous and full. It was not a young face; the telltale wrinkles of age had already laid the shape of character upon it and depicted a young matron, perhaps of some thirty cycles or so. A strong face and not unattractive. She—as Dirshan was content to now know her—was smiling. "It pleases me that I be called Iyali, for it is a woman's name. And the explanation for my presence will be that I am your free companion, come across the mountains to join you. I am sure it will satisfy any possible question. Gett will readily believe it; indeed, he does so already."

Dirshan was about to say more, but at that moment Gett returned, tugging at his breeks, and settled down in the circle of warmth. "It is lucky for us that Iyali was able to find this spot," he said. "This waste is almost trackless with all this snow. Rema showers fortune on us all."

Dirshan shrugged and accepted the obvious. "Yes, I was tired last night or would have thought to offer some sacrifice for it. Remind me when we have the opportunity and something to offer besides dried meat." He switched subjects. "I see, Gett, that you undid my pack. What think you of that sow bear now that it's dead?"

"A mighty beast, though I can also see you did not get off without being marked. I'll have to tend to it before we leave—I have some ointment in my pack. But as for the bear, I have seen sea beasts a hundred times that size, with teeth to match the size." He did not add that they were usually not hunted with an ax. "A goodly trophy. But it is best that we are high enough up for the cold. Already the skin starts to smell; in the heat it would quickly rot. The claws and teeth one can save . . . as for the rest, back in the pit there."

Dirshan laughed thinly. "Compared to some of the swill I ate aboard that League galley when I met you, this would smell sweet. But the cold will keep it well enough until we return and show it to those of my clan. The teeth and claws will go to my brother's sons so that they know they are avenged." He helped himself to a bowl of steaming stew which was bubbling on the fire, speaking anew from around the edges of the hot broth as he waited for it to cool. "I think we should leave these highlands as soon as possible and go down to the road. Already the new moon waxes full, and we have but one horse to the three of us. Ke'in will be waiting for us at the meeting place, with whatever members of my clan he may have gathered and some new information. After we finish, break camp." This was addressed to Gett. "We should be low enough by tonight so that this snow will abate." Iyali said nothing, but Dirshan did not miss the quick and fleeting grin which passed over her features. Dirshan again remembered her comment about the torque. It was a cold bundle which rested in his pouch.

Before another hour had passed, they were off, after Dirshan's wounds were bound. Dirshan and Gett were afoot, with Iyali and the packs on the remaining horse. She had not demurred when he ordered her to climb on; though for some reason—perhaps the set of her mouth before she again pulled up the concealing hood—he had had the distinct impression that she was again laughing. That was only one more thing to add to a growing list of irritations, about which he could do nothing.

Dirshan pushed them hard once they reached the lower lands, for the snow was less and he wanted to make up for the lost time now that they no longer had to trail the bear. As before, they encountered few people; most avoided them and went about their own business. They talked with no one. The days went past slowly—up at dawn, push on for as long as the light or an easily followed trail could be seen, and then another fire for the night. Small storms seemed to plague them, almost as if the mountain were taking out its wrath on the departing trespassers, but as they passed on, it faded away in the short distance, as if it were sent only to bother them. Dirshan was again reminded of the conversation of the first night he had returned to the base camp, when he had been told that the torque was a means of drawing storms. He had been inclined to ignore it, but perhaps it was true. At least the one time he had taken it out and worn it over his broad chest, there had been no warming of the cold metal, though his mail shirt had grown hot under the sun's rays. Even when Gett touched it, his hand had flinched, jerking back under its own accord. He had sucked his fingers for a moment, saying, "It feels like they were frostbitten. It seems a mighty charm, though useless, I think, in this cold. Out in the desert, maybe . . ."

Only one incident marred their climb down from the mountains and finally onto the narrow road which threaded through the lower foothills. The third night out, Gett, contrary to his usual practice, had arranged two sets of sleeping furs in the protection of the windbreak, but then returned to sit by the fire. His face held the same dreamy expression as it had had on the night Dirshan first talked with Iyali. On previous nights, Iyali had stayed by the fire—or at least that was what Dirshan assumed she did. This night Gett remained there. Dirshan watched in silence as Iyali came into the shelter, preparing to take her place beside him.

"No," he grunted, danger icy in his denial.

"But it would hardly be useful to act as your companion if I don't sleep with you! Besides, am I not pleasing?"

"That doesn't matter—at least now. I want no one to share my furs who does not appear as they really are. I know not exactly what you are, but perhaps it is not human. I feel that you are using me for some darkling purpose of your own, though all paths seem to run together for a while. Release Gett and return to your place." His tone was final.

"You are being foolish. I am as human as you."

"Nevertheless, I want not what you offer. Begone, or I will force you." His hand groped toward the ancient blade at his waist. It suddenly came to Dirshan's mind what an old friend and mighty wizard had once told him: You can't fight sorcery with steel. But he was determined to try.

There was a faint suggestion of a laugh in the mellow voice from out of the darkness. "You might try at that. Though I do not think you would be successful," Iyali said. "But why push what will be inevitable?" she seemed to mumble to herself.

Then, louder: "I will release Gett from his dream, though I suspect it is more pleasant than the reality he sees around him." She withdrew in silence. Dirshan was left with the feeling that he had only postponed the battle—not won it.

Five days of hard, punishing travel, and the moon was full again; a bright disk which made the night seem almost as day. The orb seemed caught in the jaws of a trap as they traveled in the growing darkness of that last night, shining as it did in the cleft which the old road followed. They would make their meeting, though perhaps two or three days late. Dirshan had assumed that Ke'in would wait. Yet his caution led him to leave his two companions on a narrow trail away from the main road, while he passed toward the meeting place himself using the footpaths over the hills. The first sentry he spotted did not even see him as he whispered past, but he did tell him that the meeting place was occupied. He bypassed the man silently and went on. It was already late, and they would have no time to waste in the thin air with its renewed bite of coldness.

As he made his way to a spot where he could see the entire valley, he passed another sentry. While he did approve of such caution on Ke'in's part, he was not impressed with the quality of his clansmen's training. Though he was a large man, he could tread quietly when necessary; but he was surprised at the apparent laxness which allowed him to bypass two sentries without their calling warning. They would need some patience and practice before he led them east. Carelessness often cost many lives—just possibly his own.

He finally worked himself to a knoll overlooking the spot where Ke'in had erected a camp. Though many bushes and small trees obscured his vision and the shelters below took advantage of the ground cover, the large number of campfires indicated a sizable number of men. Dirshan had not expected Ke'in to bring so many. He briefly speculated on the possibility that the clans had already risen and Ke'in had thus fallen in with some of them, leading them here. He would soon know. With some concentration, he was able to pick out one campfire which was larger than all the rest, beside which was erected a large tent. He assumed that Ke'in would be found there, along with whoever commanded this troop. Some sort of flag flapped in the wan breeze of night, but it was too far away to make out whose device was depicted there. Several figures were in the circle around the fire, and by concentrating Dirshan thought he could make out Ke'in. He had apparently succeeded in bringing up a sizable body of men. Good. It would make his work easier.

Dirshan began to ease his way back from the crest of the knoll in order to return to Gett and Iyali. Then he stopped. It would be simpler for him to go into the camp and send back a messenger for the others. He had had a long journey and was anxious for both rest and news. Nothing would be served by the extra walk in darkness. Besides, he wanted to see how close he could work himself in to the camp before he was finally challenged. It would be a good exercise.

Habitual caution made him creep from tree to bush down the hill, taking advantage of the cover as he descended. As he approached the larger fire, he could make out the figure of Ke'in, seeming to slump in sleep across from two others whom Dirshan did not recognize talking across from him. He stood erect and strode the remaining distance into camp. He would not enter his own clan creeping like a beggar come to table. Making as much noise now as he had spent in former silence, he walked into the circle of firelight.

It was a mistake which almost cost his life.

Dirshan had not been able to clearly see around the camp due to the obscuring brush which grew around it, a situation which was worse on the shallow floor of the vale. When he broke into the clearing proper, his mistake became obvious.

The two men across from Ke'in had stood to receive what was obviously an unexpected stranger; the one who did not was Ke'in. What Dirshan had thought from above to be the posture of sleep was actually secure bondage. His clan brother was slumped in a cramped position, held there by ropes and a gag in his mouth. Dirshan's first thought was that Ke'in looked extremely uncomfortable. Then a voice issued from one of the other men, both of whom had now drawn swords and faced him. "Welcome, Dirshan of the Hawk clan!" it said with heavy irony. "An unanticipated pleasure at this time of night—I would have thought to have more warning. But welcome indeed! To either captivity or death, but the choice is yours. And look around before you decide. It will be worth it."

Dirshan's reflexes were extremely well trained, and even as his mind had taken in the situation, he had already drawn both sword and dagger, slipping into his familiar fighting crouch. It had been plain in that one instant that whoever Ke'in had met in his travels, it was not his clan. He was the bait which Dirshan had freely taken. Dirshan did not recognize either of the two men who faced him; but the battle standard which waved across the fire as well as their dress confirmed what the speaker's accent had betrayed: they were from Anshan. Dirshan snatched a hasty moment to look around, judging the odds against him. What he saw told enough. Hidden in at least two of the scrubby trees about them were several crossbowmen. Two aimed for his chest. A rustle of leaves behind told him of another. He had indeed been careless. His mind flickered and dismissed the possibility of escape. Conversation would have to serve where the sword was useless.

"With honor?" He asked the one who spoke.

The other looked at him for a long moment as Dirshan sized him up, the fire flickering on the side of his face and over the carefully trimmed and oiled beard, brown banded with gray. A long linen robe completed the clothing, and golden armbands encircled the heavy and muscular arms. This speaker was a dandy, but the grip of his blade looked well worn. The other was just as obviously a soldier, perhaps with power in the ranks, but his dress showed his station. "Insofar as possible," the other said. "You may keep your weapons, but remember the trees."

With no choice, Dirshan sheathed both and came closer to the fire. Without a word to either of the two men who silently watched him, he walked over to the slumped figure of Ke'in, whose eyes now watched him with the trapped look of those who believe they have failed. Dirshan noticed that there was a dried crust of blood on the side of his head and several bruises on his face. He bent to remove the gag, but as he started to cut the bonds, the speaker said, "Leave him tied. I would not give too many targets running around for my men in the trees."

Dirshan looked at him for a second and then did as he commanded. As he bent over, he muttered in his native tongue: "Say nothing as I speak. Talk later." There was the slightest of nods. Dirshan stood erect and took a seat by the fire. If he were a captive, at least he would be comfortable. Rema only knew if Gett would have sense enough to run for cover with Iyali when he did not return to their hiding place.

While the silent man tended the fire, the other resumed his seat. His eyes never left Dirshan during that time, and his hand was firm on the sword hilt in his hand.

He finally spoke. "I have the impression that you know nothing of this. I am Heletaroy; the other is Palcin, my second. Those whom you so neatly passed in the darkness"—and then he paused, speaking to Palcin—"See that they are disciplined in the morning." Then he returned his attention to Dirshan. "They are under my command, that of the First and Second Irregular Border patrols in Anshan. We did expect to catch a fish or two in our net, but we have waited a long time for one to merely walk in on us."

"I am but a poor traveler passing on the outskirts of my homeland. I have naught to do with you or Anshan."

"Ah, that I could believe you! Unfortunately for you, though, your fellow traveler there, Ke'in, babbled a bit after he was wounded. So we knew that you, at least, would return."

"Dirshan!" Ke'in interjected, "I would not violate my—"

"Hush, boy," Heletaroy ordered. Then to Dirshan: "He is right, though it seems I could have gotten more information from him had a little torture been used. But I respect your tribesman, and he is a doughty fighter for one so young; he put two of my best out of action, and one still limps. But what he said or mumbled was enough to convince me to come this long way and to await whoever might also come here. Perhaps you have a story to tell that would interest me. If I like it, I may let you depart with your companion. If I do not, well"—he spread his hands—"then I will follow my orders."

"And they were?" Dirshan inquired.

"To scour the country from the borders of Anshan to the great north pass. Men, women, children, and beasts. They were to pass beyond the Veil, as the saying goes." Dirshan knew what it meant. Death. "A difficult order, hard to execute and unreasonable as a means to simply control a little banditry. But . . ." He spread his hands again. Dirshan had held the power of command and knew what the opposite side of the coin of responsibility was. One did as ordered, on pain of one's own head.

"I know nothing of recent matters in this land, having only recently come over the pass myself with this companion. I have been in the Empire," Dirshan told him.

"Ah yes, Alithar. Alithar the Great, Alithar the Beautiful, conqueror of the League in her last war. And an ally of my land, Anshan, though she is very far and there are many leagues between her great walls and the sand which girdles my home city. I have never seen the golden city, but what news I have had tells me that I would like to see it ere I pass the Veil. I have yet to take the road to the White Shrine. Perhaps then." He referred to the obligatory journey which all members of the Order had to undertake once in their lives.

"But why at this particular time did you chose to take the high pass to come into your land? There would be feasting and merriment along the Throat; here there is already snow on the highlands and the oncoming grip of another hard winter. I see no spoils of war on your back. Except for one tired, ragged man, there is nothing. Is that not curious?"

Even as Heletaroy spoke, Dirshan realized that he did not know as much as he had implied; he had not mentioned Gett, nor could he know of either him or Iyali some two hours down the trail. "I came to kill a bear." Without explaining more, he unslung the pack at his back, carefully unfolding it to reveal the claws which were wrapped inside. The fire gleamed from the shorn claws, lumps of dead flesh still adhering to them.

"Ah," the hitherto silent Palcin said, echoed by the other, who exclaimed, "Indeed, you are the hunter! A mighty beast wore these. It is a shame that you did not keep the skin, or is it packed, perhaps, on a horse in a hidden place? It would keep many wenches warm in the draughty air. But, all the way from Alithar? To kill a bear? Come, now."

Dirshan swiftly told them an edited version of Ke'in's quest, leaving out mention of the troubles the clans were having. He finished: "It seemed meet that I should be the one to kill this destroyer of my homeland, especially since my brother died. It was my right and duty."

"I note," Heletaroy said as he finished, "that you make no mention of the clan's rising nor of the allegiance which has gathered around this bandit named Aliffa. Perhaps you know nothing of these matters, but then . . . one does not like to take chances. And my orders were clear: after all, you still remain a tribesman." He pursed his lips.

Dirshan could almost read torture written there, for it was an order he himself might have given under the same conditions.

"Hold," he said. "We now sit over twenty leagues from the border of Anshan, unless she has grown since I was last in these parts. You must have some latitude to do as you will; yet it is plain that what you need is information. While I would not freely tell you how to destroy those of my own tribe, perhaps if I knew more of this situation, we could come to some kind of agreement. A moon has gone since I last talked with anyone in these parts. I know nothing of what may have happened. Give me leave for speech with my clan brother here and I will swear by Rema that I will not attempt an escape. Then we will talk, and thus avoid this war."

Both of the other men exchanged glances. Then Heletaroy spoke again. "You will have as long"—he bent and threw a stick of wood onto the fire—"as it takes this faggot to burn. See that your tongue is loosened in that time; otherwise its twin will go to warm the soles of your feet." Without further word, the two men rose and left the ring of firelight. The crossbowmen rested still in their perches among the trees.

"Tell me what happened," Dirshan said in a low voice.

"By the Veil, I told them nothing," the words rushed from Ke'in, his face working. "As you ordered, I went in search of those we could trust, telling all that could to meet in the Vale of Smoke, hard by the Smoking Stream. The land has been much ravaged in the time I looked for you; I have had to travel over a tenday before I saw a face I could trust. All the clans gather in the old holds, awaiting they know not what. Pain and sorrow have plainly come to our land. Rather than have all make the trek here, I passed the word to gather where I said and began my return. It was then I met this Heletaroy and his troop. They had set an ambush in the skirting road that goes around the lower hills. In my haste I fell within it; my horse fell beneath the arrows. When I finally came to my senses, it was to find myself bound and on the road to this place.

"I say to you, Dirshan, that I have said nothing when I was conscious. But who knows what passed my lips as . . . I had been aware . . . I did not fully come to my senses for three days."

Dirshan absently patted the man on the shoulder, knowing that his words could not change the guilt he plainly felt. "It could not be helped; sometimes the path we tread cannot be altered even though we know forehand the danger. Said you aught that you know of on the gathering of the clan? I would like to know more of what they do know, for plainly this captain is no fool. I see where this could be to our advantage."

"No, nothing. But I understand that this is the smaller part of his force, for once in my hearing he sent messengers to others under his command. I think they swept both sides of the roads, picking up all they could for questioning. They asked me much about Aliffa and the strength of force under him. I think that an attack on him is their real intention, or maybe this is an attempt to have the clans end him."

Dirshan sat in silence for a moment, considering alternatives as he watched the small stick burn his time away. At last he told Ke'in, "You did the best you could, and perhaps we can turn evil to our advantage. Say nothing of Gett, for it may be that he and a chance companion we picked up on the road may yet escape even if we are taken. Follow my lead when I speak. If nothing is said, they cannot fault what I will talk about. If you have a question, wait until later. Understood?"

"Yes, clan father." Ke'in bent his head in submission.

Dirshan said no more, stretching himself to relax the tension in his shoulders and ease the wound in his neck, which now itched. The stick slowly bent to a glowing ember before a figure showed on the other side of the clearing. It was Heletaroy, this time alone. "Come," Dirshan said aloud, motioning with his hands in welcome. "We must talk about our mutual problem." Swiftly and skillfully he began to outline a weaving of truth and lies to make a picture the Anshani commander would want to see.

VI

"Mutual problem?" Heletaroy murmured, seating himself. "I see only that you and your companion have a problem."

Dirshan chose his words with care. "The fact that you now hold us captive in no way affects the same problems which are before both of us. You assumed correctly that I did not return to these mountains solely to kill a bear. The troubles which have recently come to my clan had also come to my ears by the mouth of this one here, Ke'in. I left what was a high position in the Empire to see what could be done."

Heletaroy looked Dirshan over, pointedly examining his travel-worn clothes and gear. "Hmmmm," was his comment, but it sounded like a long speech.

Dirshan was a little stung. His pride had remained intact even in the high passes while trailing the sow. He reached in his pouch, reminded anew of the torque that nestled there, and removed a golden token, in appearance a coin bearing an inscription on one side and representation of Alithar on the other. He tossed it casually to Heletaroy, who caught it neatly as it spun and danced in the firelight. "Can you read the script of the Empire?" Dirshan asked.

The other man looked briefly at the coin, tilting it in the light to read it better. His face showed little except a slight widening of the eyes; but instead of tossing the coin in return, he reached out and handed it back. There was some respect in that gesture, perhaps even a little fear. "It seems I have caught a much larger fish in my net than I expected. I served the Order once, in the Chapter House in Kytheria. It is not often that one of the Family's intimates come so far south. Unless, of course," he paused, "it was stolen." Dirshan rose to his feet, action evident in his body.

Heletaroy put up his hand, adding, "But you do not look like a thief, Lord Dirshan. Sit yourself and tell your story. There appears to be more here than I thought."

Dirshan hesitated, remembering the crossbows in the darkness. He reseated himself. "I came by the token honestly, and Ke'in here can tell you of where and how he came to see me in the high city. I stand high in the counsels of the Family," Dirshan added, deeming that it would lend some weight to his words if the man before him thought Alithar was somehow involved. Even if distant, Alithar was an ally of the masters of the man who now listened. "But I left these mountains many cycles ago. Yet this is still home, even though I have an apartment in the Pillars. What needs I may have there are readily filled.

"Yet this situation was explained to me thus." And he went on to shorten the comments which Ke'in had made on their first meeting. "While this did give me great interest, it would not have been my prime consideration, nor enough to cause my leaving Alithar. Head of the Hawk clan is a worthy position"—this was for the ears of Ke'in—"but not sufficient for me to leave the center of the Empire." He said this with heavy irony in his voice and was gratified to see a slight grin on Heletaroy's face. Plainly what Dirshan had told him would not have been enough for him to leave the glories of the capital.

"Yet the situation in the Empire has stabilized in the past several moons. The League has now been removed as a threat, and the Heclos is again safe for shipping. Pilgrims can now take the water routes to the Shrine. Too long have things been left on the southern borders of the Heclos. The work of the Order was even stopped by this eternal squabble; still it is a work which should go on. Had you heard that the Isles of the Dust had fallen, north of the Shallow Sea?"

"I protect the eastern borders," Heletaroy declared, "and what news comes to me is fifth—nay, tenth-hand. It is common knowledge that there was war between League and Empire, and there was the fact that Empire triumphed. In that mix of real fact and fancy came the name of one Dirshan, who led them into victory; though I did not associate that name with you. It is a common name among the Garazi. Yours is a tale I would hear one day, but what is the effect of the fall of these Isles here at least five hundred leagues away?"

Here Dirshan began to improvise. "When the Isles fell and were forcefully converted, those chapters who took part in the original sack voted to press onward, into the Shallow Sea and its farther shores. I was not present at this, for it was a time of peril for the Empire; but I was present in council when they were discussed, and I read several of the reports. Men from that group had come unto a strange and uncouth land on this side of the Heclos. When I was raised in these mountains, my gran'fer would point east and say, 'There, where the sun rises, is an unclean land, filled with those who eat the dead.' Then there would be mention of something called the 'Black Meer' and a strange city called Cascalon."

Ke'in gasped, saying, "Why, that is the same from which come those raiders who have struck at the eastern borders! There has been rumor of great trouble with them, though that is in the clan land of the Owls."

Dirshan bid him to silence with a hand wave, concentrating his attention on Heletaroy. "Heard you aught óf this land?"

"Aye. I have even had the pleasure of fighting with them farther south. Their leader spoke of destiny in broken speech even as I had him impaled. I judged that such animals could not be converted, only killed. They are a blot on the Worlde."

Dirshan continued, "It was these same that had reached the southern edge of the Heclos and there came into contact with the Order on the march. They did drive back the advancing Order, but some information was gathered. They are now on the march westward—for flesh and *land*. It seems that the coast thereabouts is mostly barren land, and there is little there to induce them to go on unless they are ready to take to boats. But —and here is where my interest lies—they spoke of a new homeland west of the mountains. The maps in the Empire are not total blanks; the only land south of these"—he thumbed toward the looming backdrop above them—"is my home. And, of course, further west lies Anshan, though it is my home which comes first. But I do not think your masters would appreciate having these flesh-eaters, even if they raise their own as is said" —he could not keep the disgust out of his voice—"as neighbors. My interest in this information was most personal, though the Empire may be only marginally involved. Yet my interest does command some weight." Dirshan did not add—and Heletaroy did not have to have it repeated for him—that if he wished, his interest could easily be converted to total war. There were not many people who really ruled in the Empire.

"Yet the Heclos is wide, and the Empire just succeeded in winning one war. Why command the fleet and sail southward to liberate and conquer on what might possibly be only a rumor, especially since that land could not be of much use to the Empire? I would have had to explain it as a whim, but whims that move armies and fleets are expensive. Then came Ke'in. His tale of war and raiding in the highlands was of interest, especially since it joined with this other information. It presented an opportunity for me to personally investigate and perhaps forestall what might be a disaster." Dirshan paused, giving his racing mind time to think. So far he had skillfully stretched and applied the truth, and it wore on him.

"I do not make policy," Heletaroy said in the interim. "I only keep peace on the borders. But I am not stupid, and need no reader of entrails to tell me how displeased my leaders in Anshan would be to have these people"—he spat into the fire— "in place of the tribesmen here in the Range. A little raiding for sheep or women is the normal course in the Worlde. It is to be expected from . . . those who live here." Dirshan could almost have put the word "barbarian" in place of that pause. "Still, though it is possibly in the future, it is a long-term thing and not my immediate problem. Thank Rema! What my task involves is protecting the northeastern borders. There the danger at the moment comes from the clans."

He motioned around them in the darkness. "These men and

I roam far afield here; the borders of Anshan lie many leagues away. Periodic raiding from the mountains is a common thing, especially in winter, and this my men usually control; or, if I send to someone in authority in the clans, they will do it for us. There has been peace between the clans and Anshan. The yearly truce fair held in Ormelo, my headquarters, is not so much a truce as it is a mutual exchange of goods to benefit both. It also increases tax revenues." He did not add, though Dirshan was aware of it, that the money paid to Heletaroy and the troops came from these same monies before being passed on to Anshan itself. "I would have been content to leave matters as they were, even if the raiding had only increased slightly. But we have always held to the knowledge that the clans cleaved to Rema; many of the men who fought in the Name came from the clans. This excused many faults." For a moment he lapsed into the ritual tongue used in the Shrine, quoting a verse which translated meant: "To grow up within sight of city walls is to be weak, and only the strong can pass beyond the Veil." The meaning was plain to Dirshan. "Recently, however, clan raiding parties have attacked members of the Order itself! You need no instruction on what effect this will have on the relationship between the clans and Anshan. A neighbor, even though a nominal enemy, can be tolerated if he has the same religion and the same outlook on the Worlde. But some who have been captured say they have reverted to the old ways, which are stronger, and deny Order, Shrine, and even Rema!

"I anticipated what effect this report would have even as I sent it to Anshan. I can quote the reply, even as if I lay in my chamber in Ormelo: 'If the clans will not adhere to Rema, destroy them.' This, you will admit, does not give me much room. I have my own head to consider." He laughed wryly, tapping his pate with a callused hand. "Precious to me, like honey to a bear or flight to the eagle.

"So I sent out columns of hundreds, mixed equally with those officially in the Order and my regular troops. While I do not know what the others in my command have been doing, they will report to me within the next tenday. I know that I have yet to come upon anyone who does not profess a fervent love for the Order. This I suspect to be true; yet the more I travel eastward, the more sullen all become. And I note a curious fact. Except for you and your companion here, we have come upon no males capable of bearing a sword. A few of the old ones, some women, and a few boys tending sheep in the highlands. Some burned-over holds, but no *men*. You can see where that leads me?"

Dirshan nodded, seeing it plainly. At this time of coming famine and the bad season for traveling, only one reason gathers men together. War. He said as much, ending, "You then fear a march on Anshan?"

"Where else? This menace which has been mentioned in the east and to which you have added some dimension is also a possibility. Yet a convoy which was going to support a small expedition of the Order was headed for the wars in the east and thus should be considered an ally; instead it was attacked and driven back. I come to the only conclusion, and my masters the same. The habit of command is plain in your bearing. What would you do?" He sat back in his place.

The three of them gazed into the flames. In it Dirshan could see the screams of the dying, and they were his own people. He was perceptive enough to believe that the others probably saw much the same. "You have not mentioned the effect of Aliffa," he finally said.

"Because I have no firm knowledge. Declared a bandit, and with a hold somewhere in the east was my information a cycle ago. No different than ten such I could name, with but a few disgruntled followers raiding for women and something to eat. It has always been so, and the clans did more to control it than Anshan, for it was mainly the Garazi who suffered. Now"—he spread his hands—"word comes that he controls all the clans and marches west."

"Not all of them," Ke'in interjected. "The Hawks remain true to Rema, as do others. He has only the sure allegiance of the Bear. Had he not resorted to treachery . . ." Dirshan silenced him with a look.

"Ah, then you know more than I. Since we are being open and exchanging information, perhaps . . ."

"I know nothing beyond what Ke'in has told me," Dirshan said. "This member of the Bear clan—Aliffa—had begun to preach a return to the old ways and the totems. When he became dangerous, certain leaders of the other clans visited him and they were taken. He gutted them all and hanged them from the walls as a token of his good faith. My father was one of these, leaving my older brother as head of the Hawk clan. He went to take the great sow which had been ravaging the steads in the highlands and fell in her jaws. I avenged him." He kicked at the skin lying at his feet.

"Then," Heletaroy said musingly, "that makes you the clan leader for the Hawks! This becomes more intricate by the moment, like a game of Hao. But talk is dry work." He motioned the encircling trees. In the area around them Dirshan could hear the men as they came down. There was more rustling in the bushes around and behind him. A motion of Heletaroy's hand indicated to Dirshan that he should cut Ke'in's bonds, while Heletaroy bellowed: "Ho! Bring wine and meat. My guests and I would eat." It was at this point that Dirshan remembered Iyali and Gett out on the trail, but he decided to hold this close for the time. They would not be any more uncomfortable for another passage of the rising moon, and he was still in the camp of a declared enemy. Dirshan did not think that all of the crossbows had been withdrawn yet. He would not have done so.

Dirshan said no more to their host until the wine was brought; tending to Ke'in occupied most of his attention. By the way the ropes had left marks on the messenger's body, Dirshan judged that he had been tied for some time. The returning circulation must have been painful. Though low curses accompanied the return of sensation to Ke'in, most of them directed at the assorted animals in Heletaroy's parentage, Dirshan felt he had won a limited victory. He asked continued silence from Ke'in, who after the wine was brought, sat close and did not add to what was said. Dirshan had learned patience in a hard school; wisdom came only to those who acquired it.

After pledges to Order, Anshan, and the Empire, Dirshan again started serious conversation. "I see that your problem— that of stopping this raiding—is much the same as mine. I do not think that all the clans have taken up swords against the Order, for it is a belief that has served us well and has prevented much bloodshed which in the old times was all too common. My father told me of these many times in my youth, and that the Order and Rema were blessings in disguise. A return to the old ways would result only in death without gain."

"I agree," the Anshani said, "but it is argued that to prevent any trouble it would be best to destroy all. Yours would also be my counsel, but I follow orders. My position . . . is dependent upon it. I have no hereditary rank."

"But surely you know by now that even with the men you command, even if in thousands, you cannot eliminate all the clans. It would seem better to get rid of the source; this would serve your purpose as well as that of your masters."

"Indeed, I agree in principle. Anything that saves them money—such as death benefits for men killed here—serves their purpose. They are most reluctant to engage in a wholesale campaign to destroy all. I will tell you a secret. This expedition of mine was to serve only as a warning, for as you know I am already far afield. Forage is poor here."

"True," Dirshan observed. "And you will not achieve what you wish, for by your own admission, not many have fallen. Now there is this bandit, Aliffa. As you say, no more remarkable than others of that breed, but he has a following; and it seems that following grows larger every day. Not all the clans are in agreement with this proposed return to the old ways. The Order lies close to many hearts. Should this bandit be removed, I see no reason why peace cannot again be between Anshan and the clans."

Heletaroy mulled over this for a time, looking at his wine with studied concentration. Dirshan was not sanguine; this was a subtle man before him. "That is possible," he said at last, "but it has been said that his hold is far—much farther than this place is from my own homeland. And while possible elimination of this bandit would quiet my problem, the loss of my whole force in an attempt that fails . . ." He spread his hands as an aide came from the shadows and put more wood on the fire. "It would seem that I was ahead by doing only what I am ordered and letting it serve as an object lesson. No?"

"And then you would be faced with the entire strength of the clans if he gained power, for your intervention would serve only to strengthen his hold. That would not be put down simply by overrunning a few keeps in the vales. The land controlled by the clans—and much the richest—lies far to the east. As you and your men penetrate farther, you will gain nothing but increased resistance and the cementing of allegiance to Aliffa, instead of bringing an end to this hostility. How long do you wish to prolong this mutual punishment? I do not see where you would want an expedition every cycle."

"You're right. All-out war is disruptive of trade and costs my time and coin without profit. You obviously have some alternative in mind. I listen, but I promise nothing." Heletaroy sipped at his wine again.

Dirshan spoke. "From what information I have gained, I am thinking of this: On the one hand we have a bandit, outlawed but still of my people, who through fortunate circumstances rises to leadership in one of the major clans. That would not have been dangerous except that he has combined this with deceit and death, building animosity between the clans and in the end with Anshan, to the ultimate evil of fighting the Order itself. In this he appeals to several griefs among the clans." And Dirshan began to tick points off on his hand. "First, there is the everyday tension between clan and clan. Always it has been the Hawk or Bear clan who strive for primacy, with the others on one side or the other. Aliffa now leads the one, and with the death of my father has fragmented the other. This loss of balance will only result in war eventually; as it appears, he will triumph and thus he will control all. He seems well on his way to this.

"Second comes this problem of the Order. My father was still crawling when the Order came to the mountains, and many a father still remembers what was told him. In some of the deeper back vales, one still can hear of blood sacrifice for a return of the sun or luck in the hunt. The old days are remembered, when the clan totem was supreme and each claimed glory by the number of raids it conducted and treasure taken. This the Order prevented unless it was done in the Name. Many of my people do not understand this larger goal, and any one group from a Chapter House is liable to have all the clans represented. Little individual glory adheres to this.

"Lastly, there is this matter of the Ayal, the eaters-of-the-dead. I detect a larger hand here than the experience of Aliffa would call for. From what Ke'in has told me, the man is naught but an animal—clever and expert fighter at that, but not as worldly as you or I might be." Heletaroy did not smile at this left-handed compliment, taking it as truth. "That would indicate to me that there is some outside force. Only one party stands to gain from this war between Order, Anshan, and the clans. Only the Ayal. I already know they march west. The only wall which would prevent them from advancing would be the Order, which in years past would come to the aid of the clans if only because so many of the men in it call the Range their homeland. Yet with Anshan and Order fighting at the rear and the Ayal poised to take the remains piecemeal . . . Even a child has the power to remove a hill of sand a grain at a time." Dirshan was quiet.

"The pieces fit this plan. If this, then, is the case, what do you see to do?"

"That with these you have in your command, along with those clansmen as I can claim leadership to, we march and pull down this Aliffa. Some of yours will die, as will some from the clans. But I see that it is better to face him and the flesh-eaters together than go under the knife one body at a time. And both of our problems would be solved."

"Yet there are some flaws in this crystal, Dirshan, which you have not mentioned. I am aware that the farther I forage into clan territory, the more risk I run of pitched battle or ambush. Yet there is no guarantee that those not aligned with Aliffa would come over with me or you, for I have done some damage to their lands. Your reputation has come before you, and I have your word to assist me. But there is still the responsibility I have to Anshan. It would have to be a clearly won victory that I bring home to report; anything else is failure. Now, to do what you propose would be to put all on one throw of the knucklebones, a risk which does not at the moment appeal to me. As you said, you know nothing of the recent affairs in the clans now. All you have done is kill a sow bear. You see the problem?"

"Ke'in, tell him what you saw and did on your journey east at my orders." The youth spent five minutes detailing what had been accomplished under Dirshan's direction, finishing with: "They are gathering now. With a new, strong leader to guide the clan, they will gladly join in pulling down Aliffa. But this they would do with or without your help," he added. There was plain disapproval in his speech, which Dirshan understood to be a reflection of his dislike of the venture when combined with the forces of Heletaroy.

Dirshan ignored this, preferring to strengthen his own argument with the Anshani leader. "In addition to this, you should not spurn this skin before me. Leadership among the clans is not solely based on the visible; there is also the favor of one's totem. The death of my brother in the jaws of this beast seemed to prove the ascendency of the Bear clan, fragmenting whatever opposition would form. The sow is dead. I myself will throw the head skin of it into the face of Aliffa. It will seem to many that he has, in fact, lost the favor of even his own god. It is well known that I joined the Order many cycles ago and continued to fight for Rema. My reputation is worth ten troops of a thousand, for men are really what they believe in.

"And I will give you one more proof of my intention to join our interests without guile. An hour's journey afoot down the backtrail wait two people; one my leman, the other my sworn companion, Gett." Dirshan tightened his hand slightly on Ke'in's shoulder to prevent any reaction—the man knew nothing of Iyali. "Should I have wished to play you false, I could have merely remained silent and let them carry word of my capture to the clans. I do not think that you could even fight off the united fury of even the Hawks in an attempt to gain my release. Even should you win and I die, your forces would be so reduced that you would have to return to Anshan—and with some losses to explain."

Heletaroy made no comment for a moment, then snapped his fingers. An aide came out of the shadows. He was given swift commands to go out and return with Dirshan's companions and rapidly left to do this bidding. Heletaroy smiled ruefully at Dirshan and said, "If it is as you say and they do wait, I will consider seriously what you propose. It is neither safe nor sane, but what on this side of the Veil is?

"But while we wait let us play another game. Play you Hao? It will serve to pass the time."

"Aye, agreed," Dirshan replied, expelling his breath, not realizing that he had been holding it. "But I will take the red and black. I feel more comfortable in the attack."

"As I on the defense, for it is the safer game." Another aide came swiftly on Heletaroy's command, leaving to return with a leather bag containing the pieces and an inlaid ivory board. In the firelit dead of night they settled down to play, whiling away the time of decision.

VII

It was morn on the following day. Dirshan and the commander from Anshan had played the ancient game for three passes, Dirshan winning the first and the third. The game itself was the passion of many of the members of the Order, perhaps because the pieces and moves were based on the structure of the religion and its origins were said to have dated from the time of the Prophet. Heletaroy was an excellent player, but the advantage between two good players usually rested solely on who had the first move. Before going on to their respective furs the night before, they had discussed playing at some time when they would have leisure to look over their moves—perhaps in Anshan itself. Dirshan took this to be an excellent sign—in order to play, he would have to be alive.

Midway through the third game, the patrol which the man had dispatched returned, bringing with it Gett and Iyali along with the horse and its packs. The commander from Anshan had simply raised an eyebrow when introduced to Iyali, and there was plain curiosity in his features. Ke'in had been cautioned not to act surprised at the sight of her, so he did not react. Gett was ignored, a fact which was noted by Dirshan and almost provoked an outburst that was stifled by a "In the morning!" Dirshan had the others set up camp a little away from the fire, out of earshot. He wanted nothing to disturb his newfound companion and the troop commander; he still felt that they were prisoners.

When Dirshan returned to the tent which had been erected for their use, he found both Gett and Iyali still awake. He said a few words about their position to both, with a caustic comment caused by fatigue directed at Iyali and her ability to see into the future. "To be sure," she answered cryptically, "but you will need Heletaroy and he you. What would it boot us to warn you, knowing that you probably would not enter the camp out of caution?" She then lapsed into a silence neither wished to disturb. Gett had little to offer, besides the fact that he had soon thought that something was wrong and had hidden at the side of the road. When the patrol had come and called out, he had joined them. "What else was I to do, without fire or a warm bed companion?" Dirshan agreed and sent him to his furs, following almost immediately. His thoughts needed rest, and he anticipated more trouble on the morrow.

It was midmorn before Heletaroy strolled into their camp, a courtesy which Dirshan appreciated since he had wisely decided to stay in his furs until he had to get up. While he and his companions were still in the hands of an enemy, at least they were relatively safe. A rested body was of more use than nimble wits if there was fighting to be done.

"Hola!" Heletaroy said, entering the camp with Palcin, his second, trailing behind. His companion looked no more savory by daylight—an impression which was not helped by the red scar that ran along his jaw—but the Anshan commander had found some time to bathe. Indeed, his robes would not have looked out of place in Anshan itself, and somewhere he had contrived to have his beard trimmed, forked, and oiled. Dirshan had the suspicion that it had been some time since he had last seen a woman, even if another man's. But if it was to his advantage . . . "The sun promises fair to drive off some of this chill," Heletaroy continued. "What do you say to more conversation in my tent? Some specifics this time."

Dirshan agreed, adding as an aside to Gett, "Clean up and see what aid Ke'in might need. Do not leave the camp." Dirshan did not give a reason why; though Gett was very cunning and curious. He trusted him to obey.

Heletaroy's quarters were as Dirshan expected; the tent twice the size as the others and furnished much as he would have seen in the Anshani's home in Ormelo. The silk underlay which lined the walls was exquisite, much the finest work he had seen even in the Empire. He commented on it, Heletaroy preening in obvious satisfaction. "I . . . um . . . liberated it from a trader in the west. A tax matter, I believe. A gift . . . of sorts." He smiled knowingly to Dirshan, who nodded while pursing his lips.

Around a makeshift table, they toasted each other's health and that of their respective homelands before getting around to the real business, which commenced with Heletaroy's "And now let us talk of Aliffa and his group of bandits." He looked at Dirshan expectantly.

"My proposal is short, but I think it will be effective to obtain our mutual goal. Your orders are to prevent the raiding and suppress a possible revolt against the Order. To this end you have been sent out to scour the area and act as a reminder in case there is a larger buildup of the clans. The fear is that they may try to invade Anshan. Am I correct?"

"Yes, in the main. Though I have not been very successful at that. As I admitted last night, most of my men have been successful in riding to and fro collecting sheep. Still, those were my orders. I can't control whom I run into in the process."

"My purpose is akin to yours, then. I want to prevent possible bloodshed before it is war between the two of us. I include myself because I am now, for the moment, clan leader of the Hawks. I say that the cause of this trouble lies in Aliffa and those he has gathered to himself under the false belief that he has overridden the Order and opens up a new time of dominance for the clans. If he were removed, I believe this futile raiding would cease; those who had gone over to him would return to both Order and their clans. I will not concern myself with the Ayal just yet; that is a matter which can be worried about when it looms."

"Then what you propose is a joining of forces—myself and my men along with whatever strength the loyal clans can bring to bear. Feasible, though it would require some planning. But there are some flaws. The first lies in your ability to gain the support of the clans—will they follow you? You are but a lone man, with some admitted call on their allegiance, but I wonder how complete that is. I have a thousand men in this area of the country." Dirshan nodded; it confirmed his estimate and Ke'in's. "Which is a small force, to be sure, but powerful enough to prevent even a large raiding party. They are under one command, and many of them believe they fight apostates.

"Another reason is more personal. My orders were to ride as far as the great pass over the Northern Range and thence scour the land for five leagues on either side of the road to as far as three days east. We are doing that now. When my men return, I can go back to Anshan, my superiors will be satisfied, and I can rest for a while in well-earned ease. Instead of riding my accursed-to-Rema animal which does naught but give me boils on my arse. To go who knows how many leagues farther, on your word, for what might only be an empty field of death . . . I think you see the point.

"Do not mistake me. I am impressed by your presence. I have heard of you from afar, like a star which has receded into the horizon and there gleams as a beacon for all." Heletaroy chuckled grimly. "And the exploit you propose—well, it would repair what has come to be a somewhat tarnished reputation in certain quarters in Anshan itself. There is no better cure for whispers than the loud voice of victory. But to take the chance . . . Ahh, I regret that I have lost the fire of my youth. I learned early that glory is purchased only through blood, and it could be yours—or, more to the point, mine. What proofs or inducements can you offer me?"

Dirshan rejoiced in his heart; in judging the man, he had struck the best chord. Heletaroy was not a coward, but the line between it and prudence was one he crossed only reluctantly. "Send Palcin to get Ke'in. Then, if you have a map, I think I can make this plan more practical for you." Heletaroy called out the command and Dirshan continued. "I wish only one thing at the moment: the unity of my people and thus to the Order when this invasion I foresee comes. Yet, as Ke'in will tell you, Aliffa has a stronghold in the east and has been there for some cycles. I wish only to have the man; what booty may fall our way means nothing to me. If all of it were to disappear on your return to Anshan . . . It would be a matter for you and your masters in the capital. Consider it a payment for your help, as well as the additional benefit that you have resolved this thorn in their sides."

Heletaroy answered directly. "A bribe? What is this you offer a commander and soon to be provincial governor?" There was some heat in his voice, moderated by the slight smile in his voice and bearded face. "Yet as payment for the troops, and with some sent along to smooth a few palms in the capital . . ." He mused silently for a moment, then continued, "Yet it would do much to quiet those rumors I spoke of earlier, and then I could retire to my well-earned ease, away from the complications of borders and this possibility of strife."

He made his decision. "Bargain then, and we will drink on it. Whatever of value is recovered, I will take to Anshan on my return. Whoever chooses to return to the allegiance to clan and Order you may have; as for the rest . . . some I will take with me as proof of my triumph. The rest will be put to the sword. Their presence will be safe for neither of us; either at my back when I return or around you if you are fighting this other enemy. Agreed?" He raised his half-filled cup.

Dirshan looked at him for a moment, then clinked cups and drained his. They looked at each other and grinned. Two wolves look much the same over a carcass before proceeding to devour it piecemeal. Dirshan's only worry was that there might not be enough booty to satisfy Heletaroy's greed, but he was satisfied that until then they could work together. Each recognized what drove the other; it was the way of the Worlde that neither wished to change.

Palcin, followed by Ke'in, entered the tent just as the two of them were looking over the painstakingly drawn parchment which Heletaroy had spread on the table. Palcin looked a bit disconcerted at his leader's evident state of mind, but he did not comment. Following orders had made him what he was; he saw no reason to change.

After words from Dirshan, Ke'in said, "The clans which are

loyal have been told to meet here, hard beside the ford which crosses the Smoking Stream after it comes out of the Red Cleft. I chose that as the place because it is central to many of the Hawk holds, and it is the traditional meeting place for important business among the Garazi.

"Besides the Hawks there will be some others. This taking by Aliffa of four clan chiefs has caused a call for feud and many thirst for his blood. I spread the word that you, Dirshan, had returned and gone to seek the great sow bear which had taken your brother. Many left immediately to follow my bidding, some as messengers to pass the word that there would soon be a Council to pass on this matter." There was pride and glee in his voice as he continued. "Now that you have taken the dreaded beast, there will be no trouble in gaining a following from every vale, big and small. That sow bear was looked upon as a mighty totem and was pointed out as the strength of the Bear clan. Its death alone will do much to dispel the hold Aliffa had on many; it will show he does not have the favor of the old ones as he claims. You are looked upon as if you were the Order itself, and now you have triumphed."

"How many do you think will be there in—let us say five days from this morn?" Heletaroy asked.

Dirshan nodded at a very puzzled Ke'in, who replied, "It has been almost thirteen days since I rode west, and it would take at least five or six of heavy riding to reach the ford and the Smoking Water—more if the weather comes early while we are still close to the mountains. Many will not be reached yet; but of the Hawks I would expect at least three hundreds, and a sizable number of others once the news has gone out. Many will arrive late; they will not take the road because rumor of your coming has made all cautious. If word is left for all to follow, they will come. Not less than a thousand—perhaps fifteen hundreds would ride out and join.

"Yet speed is important, and not because of the weather. Aliffa has many who do not openly join him, but would as readily report any movement along the road if they thought they could profit later. It cannot be held secret that others in the clans march on him. We can expect them to be ready. Unfortunately, they are already provisioned for the season to come, and they will be within their own hold."

"Let's worry about that chasm when we approach it, not fifty leagues away," Dirshan interjected. "How are the roads and vales from the Smoking Water to Aliffa's hold? And how many might oppose us?"

"This map"—Ke'in pointed to several blank spots on the right marked with the conventional ideogram for the unknown —"is not complete. The road wends along the hills, this way"— he traced it with his finger—"and then comes over the Smoking Water at the second ford. It is gravel there. Farther down it is impassable without rafts and not at all during the spring when the snow melts in the highlands. From the ford east, it is another four-day journey before one turns into the hills, and much of that must be on foot. A horse will refuse to take the trails when mounted—they are too steep. Say, three days from the road before one is in sight of the hold. I saw it last cycle during the solstice, when your father entered the gates to his death. There is another path which can be seen coming in from the east behind the hold, but a deep chasm separates a path to it. Where it goes I have no knowledge, for that land is little known to me. Perhaps one could find a guide; it is the land of the Snow Owls, and they have no love for Aliffa.

"His strength in numbers is harder to judge. The hold itself is huge; almost a small town built into the rock face of a cliff. He has the allegiance of the Bear as well as others who have turned outlaw. Landless men, mercenaries, those who flee to escape a just penalty . . . Perhaps two thousands altogether—he has been recruiting these for over three cycles. Not all could stay within the hold. Perhaps not even Aliffa is there—I heard it said that he had been raiding in the south."

Heletaroy looked down at the map, pacing off the distance with his fingers as he counted slowly with his lips. "Roughly equal in force, then, because I have to leave some here and others are still on the road and have too far to return . . . but I think it can be done. Palcin"—his captain almost snapped to attention at the tone in his commander's voice—"give orders to break camp—all except for twenty who will remain for whoever returns. I'll give them their orders later." He stepped to the door for a moment and looked up at the sun. "Pull in the western pickets. Send scouts east along the road. Have all report here in twenty minutes. We ride within an hour after high sun —I want to be on the road by then."

Palcin departed as Heletaroy turned to Dirshan. "We shall have five leagues behind us by camp tonight; speed will count in this game. Your party will ride with me—in front, in case we come upon any of your clansmen. They are liable to regard us with little love. I'll send an orderly to your tent—he'll see that you get horses. And Dirshan"—he paused in heavy emphasis— "we have struck a bargain, you and I. I trust you will feel comfortable riding to my right?"

Dirshan laughed without mirth. He looked at Heletaroy's costume, knowing by the man's remark that whatever his dress, he had earned the rank he carried. "Where else?" he replied, and with Ke'in left the tent.

Back in their own tent, Dirshan spent some time telling the others of the agreement he had made with Heletaroy, leaving aside mention of the bargain he made over any possible treasure. Ke'in would certainly object, though he might go along with it for the clan's sake; Gett would be indifferent to what he considered the way of the Worlde; and Iyali—well, Dirshan did not know what to make of their traveling companion and of her opinions. He had not bothered to explain to Ke'in where she had come from and trusted that the man would not bother to ask. What his clan chief did was his business; he would have backed him against any odds.

As Ke'in and Gett went to repack their goods on horses which had arrived at Dirshan's request, Iyali hung back. "Do not fear Heletaroy," she said, "but watch Palcin. He is the ear of Anshan in his master's tent. Do not be misled by his taking orders."

Dirshan, hands on his hips, stared at her for a second. "I did not need your warning, since you saw fit not to do so as I was placing my head into a snare last night. Whence comes this tidbit of information? Does your power as a seer extend to little things like this, or can you also see what is plain to any discerning eye?" Dirshan was a little disgusted with her and her unasked-for aid.

"Your bitterness is unwarranted, and I will ignore it. You could hardly have removed Aliffa yourself, and these of Anshan offered a chance for help. What good would it have done for me to remind you or warn away, since it was plain that you would come out best in the end? The future is a weaving of scattered threads. Just because I can pick out an occasional piece of the warp does not mean I see the whole pattern, which is too big to see so close to it. I told you that the seeing eye has grown dark so close to the time. I warn you of Palcin because it seemed needful, not because I think you cannot see it." She walked away haughtily.

All set out that afternoon under a sun which had turned watery, a bleak and drear time which was only fitfully relieved by some faint trace of greenery as they descended into a tiny vale and crossed a creek. The first day and two following passed without much conversation among those in the lead party. Most of their concentration was spent in riding along the narrow road, pushing their horses as hard as possible before it was necessary to either stop for a meal or final camp for the night. The mountains had begun to curve away to the left as the days passed, and the weather turned slightly warmer. At least to Dirshan, Heletaroy showed an unexpected fortitude for travel as the days passed. He spent much of his time recounting tales of his travels as a youth in the service of the Order. Dirshan was sensible enough to know that this was directed at Iyali, but he said nothing of it because he expected it and thought it served to lighten the journey. He did consider telling Heletaroy that she was a little old for his attentions, by what he thought was at least a factor of twenty, but he refrained. It made the trip interesting and allowed him time for his own thoughts and plans. Aliffa and what might happen in the final moment weighed heavily on his thoughts, as did the torque which now and then rattled in his pouch to remind him of its presence. He had not yet questioned Iyali as to its use, although she slept in the tent beside him. He had little to say to her. He was somewhat afraid of what she might know of the future, and he preferred to face each day without knowledge of what would happen. It made each new experience different. Besides, he was in his homeland, and each new bend in the road brought back memories of his youth.

No one passed them on the road in the first two days, which Dirshan expected in a land that prepared itself for war. Isolated reports of the far-ranging scouts did speak of some activity in the hills to either side, the sight of someone who was shadowing their movements. Since Heletaroy did not give it much worry, Dirshan did not comment; though had he commanded, he would have sent someone out at night to circle and possibly capture a prisoner for information. But they were not his men.

They had been riding for some hours on the morn of the fourth day, the halfway point well behind them, when they came upon their first traveler. It was an old man, a follower of the Nothe sect, with a jingle of bells that preceded him even as did his odor of unwashed sanctity. The people in the lead party pulled aside to let him pass. Some of the more pious of the troops threw bits of food and coins at the old man's feet. His crazed eyes glaring from under coarse and unwashed locks did not pay them attention. All interest was in the unseen as he hopped from one foot to another and passed them. They watched as the man disappeared out of sight around a bend, making his way on foot to the distant Shrine perhaps two thousand leagues away. Dirshan wondered if he would succeed and how many times he had made this journey before.

It was Palcin, riding at Heletaroy's left, who spoke first. "I sometimes wonder if the Prophet had this intention when he founded the Order. To walk continuously to and from the Shrine—it seems a waste. Once is an obligation; the rest . . ." He shrugged.

Dirshan would not have commented, except that this was one of the few times he had heard the man volunteer anything.

"Perhaps he sees things we do not. When I served the Order, such a one stopped with us for the night. His vision was good, though at the time I doubted his strength equal to the task he had set himself to. But he was true to his vows and ate no meat, only grain. He had killed his brother by accident; it was his way of salving blood guilt."

"And probably preventing himself from being killed in a blood feud," Gett said cynically. "I distrust any man whose sole purpose is to see beyond the Veil before his time. When Rema gives the call, yes; but there is much to do beforehand. Why waste one's life, which is given to be used, before it becomes necessary?"

Heletaroy chimed in. "Aye, it is wise not to take one's religious obligations too seriously. But it is an interesting problem —I mean the argument between such mystics and those of— how shall we term it?—a more practical bent? Nothe preached that since life is naught but a preparation for passing beyond the Veil. Only the express prohibition of the Prophet against self-killing led him to preach total dedication in this ideal to his followers. The other side of the argument stresses that only our time in the Worlde earns us a place beyond; that if we were not meant to accomplish anything, we would not find ourselves here in the first place. Thus one should do as much as possible to not only improve himself, but also to spread the belief as widely as possible. Through force—using the Order—if necessary.

"Personally, I am a skeptic. I am born, I serve the obligations of Rema, and when I die, I shall see what is on the other side of the Veil. Beyond that I see only the necessity that I die naturally, with a fervent wish for old age and plenty of good food and drink. What does the other half of the faithful think of this, Iyali?"

The woman was silent for some time, during which they trotted east slowly. Finally: "I do not think that Rema would care one way or the other what males do with their lives. Should you die tomorrow or pass beyond the Veil fifty cycles hence, it matters little to the place you leave or the one you will take up.

Live life as you wish; you will eventually die." Then she was silent, though her comment had a definite dampening effect as
they rode on in silence. Dirshan almost shivered, perhaps because of the way Iyali pronounced the Name. It was in the
tone one used for the living and not for the highest belief in
the Worlde; almost as if one discussed the follies of a loved
and dear friend, whose faults one knew. He did not like it.

This day they had also began to pass into and through the
first of the rounded hills that began to peak around them,
forming part of the drainage basin which fed the Smoking River
beyond them. For the most part, the road followed the lower
sections of the land, rising only when a hill would have completely blocked passage east. Several times they splashed
through small creeks wending their ways through the lower
ground, walls of half-leaved trees in the small valleys warnings
as they came up to them. They crossed another hillock and descended into another valley when suddenly Dirshan checked
his horse and brought it across to partially block Heletaroy and
Palcin. "We have had no scouts' reports in some time. I would
rather wait until we knew something of the land afore us before going on."

"Perhaps you are right," Heletaroy answered, staring at the
hills around them. "These hills do seem to frown, perhaps only
brooding on old injuries. And we knew that we were watched;
we all heard the reports." He peered down the road as it snaked
down the hill fringed with vegetation, crossed what must have
been a sizable creek below, and then climbed the other slope to
disappear as a narrow thread on the crest.

His "Let's wait until . . ." was suddenly cut off by a harsh
scream from the brush above and beside them. There was a
sudden humming like scattered bees around their party, the
muted hiss of passing arrows. In a brief fragment of stopped
time, Dirshan saw an arrow pierce the neck of Palcin's horse,
watched it rear as its teeth drew back in a cry of mortal pain
and then tossed its rider. Without a moment's hesitation Dirshan had drawn his short sword and forced his animal toward
the source of the screams. Yelling "Ambush!" at the top of his

mighty lungs, Dirshan jumped the beast off the road and into the brush and trees, taking the battle to their yet-unseen attackers. There was a milling pause. Then the rest of the forward party who were still mounted urged their horses into following him.

VIII

Once he broke through the thin screen of brush which lined the right side of the road, Dirshan paused for a moment. His breakthrough into the brush had put him beside one of the hidden archers. As this man turned, his face a mass of surprise by the suddenness of Dirshan's appearance, Dirshan casually reached out and decapitated him. He hardly stopped to see where the headless trunk fell. That death gave him a moment to survey their position and see what chance they had to evade this ambush.

Now that Dirshan was off the road, he could see how narrowly they had escaped disaster. The road had just topped a crest and was following the line of the slope down into another valley. At the bottom he could see a small, hurrying stream and what was obviously a ford; the stream itself lined with trees that still bore the color of late fall. Here and there he could pick out moving men. The ambush had been laid out in the classical manner: one line paralleled the moving line of troops and the other met it at right angles and across the front of their march. Yet Dirshan had no time to casually admire its quality; arrows still skipped and danced in the air, and even as others in the forward party followed him into the brush, he realized that he could no longer sit there. A sudden whoosh of an arrow past his face made a stronger point, as did the din of dying men in the area behind him.

Dirshan looked right and left, wondering where the main force of their enemies was located. A small knot of men could be seen on the slope above them, at least one of whom was waving wildly to someone out of his sight. He quickly looked for a way to climb the steep slope, his mind wondering if the beast beneath him could make it, when Heletaroy broke through and came alongside.

While the commander of the Anshani may have appeared the perfect courtier in his clothes, his blade was now in his hand, and there was bloodlust in his face. "Where are they?" he screamed above the din as behind them came the sound of a horn as his second warned those behind them.

"Some right, some left!" Dirshan cried. "Let them be taken from behind. Let's take the top!" And he motioned with his sword toward the position above them, already forcing the horse to mount the slope before them.

Heletaroy delayed only long enough to shout at Palcin before he kicked his animal into action behind Dirshan. The two made heavy going as they tried the slope.

They would not have made it—Dirshan's horse already had a flesh wound in the withers which caused it to rear in pain—had he not suddenly come upon a narrow path running around and up the slope of the hill. One man stood at that point, a spear poised in his hand for flight; but Dirshan did not check his horse as he rode him down. He scarcely noticed that the form was a bloody corpse even as he went past to mount the trail.

The entire sequence of events from the time that Dirshan had felt danger took almost an eyeblink, and it was plain that the speed of their reaction had destroyed the effectiveness of the attack. The trail the two men followed wandered upward, and it was impossible for those above not to know of their approach. Dirshan half-expected them to mount and flee even before they came upon them since their attack was an obvious failure. But it was not to be so. When Dirshan finally crested the hill and stood for a moment to look over the men there, he saw them waiting, weapons in hand.

In that brief time, he saw six men who waited even as he goaded his animal into action with the flat of his blade. The horse leaped explosively beneath him, surging forward at a dead run. Dirshan kept his head low and close to its neck as they raced forward, his short sword extended at his side. With Heletaroy at his side, their first pass broke apart the group afore them as wind scatters the leaves of a dead autumn. Then they were in the midst of their attackers, hacking at the men who stumbled out of the way of their assault.

On the first pass, Dirshan had speared a man with the look of a tribesman; he died with the sword embedded in his chest. Dirshan finally checked his animal, violently pulling back on the reins so that it reared. Dirshan used its weight to pull the blade free. Yet the hilt, slippery with the dead man's blood, was jerked out of his hand. At the midpoint of the horse's upward leap, a spear, aimed for where Dirshan's chest would have been, took the animal full in its side. The blow killed the horse instantly. In the moment of frenzy, as it twisted away from the point of pain in its chest, the animal fell backward, pinning Dirshan's leg under its heaving body and trapping him.

The shock of the fall dazed Dirshan for a moment, though his head snapped aside instinctively as the spear came down again and narrowly missed his face. Dirshan was aware that Heletaroy was still horsed, but he could spare little interest as the spearman drew back for another thrust. Dirshan lunged out with his hand, his fingers closing on the shaft slightly behind the crossguard which prevented it from passing through its target. Grimly holding on as his attackers cursed and jerked at his weapon, Dirshan let him partially pull him out from under the still-feebly-kicking animal. Then his attacker did the sensible thing and dropped the spear, but not before Dirshan switched hands and grabbed one of the feet which had been kicking him in the chest as he lay.

Wasting no time in niceties Dirshan snatched at the greasy leg, finally getting purchase on the kneecap. With a wrench of his hand, he ripped and tore at the vulnerable spot. There was a tearing sound, then a popping noise that was audible above the clashing metal. The man above him screamed as his leg gave way beneath him. Dirshan fished about at his waist and pulled out his dagger, the ancient blade plunging upward into the falling man above him. The keen edge pierced the artery inside the leg. Even as he died, the man twisted and fell away, allowing Dirshan to pull himself out from under the horse.

He stood erect as he surveyed the scene atop the hill. Three of the six men who had been there were now down. The others had drawn together, forming a tight knot that bristled with spear points. They had succeeded in keeping Heletaroy, who was still mounted, away; though he was drawing a narrow circle around them to keep them from escape. The danger of his charging them was evident, even from Dirshan's position five rods away. In a moment when Heletaroy guided his animal forward and too close one of the attackers' spears darted out and scored a slipping tear in the animal's side. Heletaroy backed his mount away, content for the moment to contain his opponents. His face was drawn into the rictus of death, the teeth visible as the lips drew back. There was much blood on the flowing white robe which was girdled about him.

Now that the immediate heat of battle was gone, Dirshan was content to look over the three men. One seemed to be a member of the hill clans, as his leather breeks, size, and gray-tinged hair proclaimed. The other two were such as Dirshan had not seen before. Both had dark skin, yet not dark enough to obscure the whorls and lines of blue embedded in the skin of their faces. He had seen the like before—deep in the ice cavern in the mountains behind him. A battle shirt of heavy-forged links backed with leather hung to the knees of each, and each wore a helmet with metal fringes at back and sides. An ax hung from the left side of the belts, and white necklaces waved to and fro on their chests as they moved. Instead of fierce war cries which Dirshan would have expected, they were deathly quiet. They simply watched both him and Heletaroy with the same lack of expression, eyes watching, watching Heletaroy mounted on the moving horse and then Dirshan in his silence.

"Hai! Hai!" Heletaroy yelled over the sound of his animal's drumming hooves, trying to tempt one of them to break their formation. He had no takers. Finally he saw Dirshan as he stood, shouting to him: "So, you still live, eh? What say you that we leave these carrion to the stickers of my men below? They'll have a longer reach, and we'll not break this ring without help."

Dirshan did not reply. Instead, he retrieved his blade from the chest of the first man he killed. He grunted in fatigue as he braced his foot to pull it out, shaking the blood free as he did so. Then, striding outside the circle described by Heletaroy's horse, he came abreast of the man who appeared to be also of the Garazi. "I am Dirshan," he said, addressing him with a salute of his sword, "Master of the Hawks and a man of these hills. I offer you a return to Rema with the honor of your clan or an honorable death at my hand." He motioned with his sword to a place before him, away from the other two men. "Which choose you?" he asked.

The man licked his lips nervously, looking from right to left at the men beside him. The appearance of Dirshan afore him, covered in blood and bulking huge in his wrath, joined to the sure death that even now was climbing the hill in the form of Heletaroy's troops, convinced him. His "A return to Rema" was cut short by convulsive jerking as the man to his right barely moved, his one hand a blur of steel that plunged deep into the other's kidneys. Even as the hill man dropped, the other two men moved back to back, ignoring the jerking corpse beneath them. Both watched impassively as Dirshan and Heletaroy stared at them.

"So," Dirshan murmured as he walked around them, "at least one of you speaks the language of the hills. I offer both of you the same terms. Which do you choose?" Neither of them answered, but even as Dirshan looked over to Heletaroy, he noticed a break in the stance of the man to his right. Even as the spear rose, Dirshan screamed at Heletaroy: "Don't kill both— we need information!" as he ducked to one side and ran low toward the two men.

The man to the right was quick. Even as Dirshan came in, ducking so that the expected throw would pass over him, the man checked his swing, bringing the weapon around to spit Dirshan as he rushed forward. Dirshan twisted aside, almost backing into the two men, and brought down the blade he carried on the spear. The heavy steel snapped the haft of the weapon directly behind the point. Dirshan let his momentum carry him forward, slamming into the two men. Like two rocks struck by another they bounced aside, with Dirshan between them.

The man to the right was the better fighter, for even as his spear was broken, he dropped it, snatching at the ax which hung from his belt. Dirshan could have killed him at that moment, but he wanted at least one alive. As the man half-bent to tug at the snagged weapon, Dirshan kneed him in the stomach, buffeting him aside with his hand as the man started to fall. The other man, who had been surprised by the swiftness of Dirshan's attack, had backed away so as to have freedom with the longer spear he still carried. As he drew back to thrust, Dirshan fell forward and continued to roll on his shoulder, rolling to his feet several steps beyond.

But Dirshan did not pause. He well knew that the secret to any attack was speed. He waited only long enough for his feet to go beneath him before jumping at the man again. His opponent misjudged the timing of his stroke—or perhaps the position he assumed Dirshan would take—and it passed harmlessly over him. Dirshan dropped his sword and came in low to tackle the man around the legs, upending him on his back.

The impact stunned the man, for he lay face up for a moment with Dirshan sprawled at his feet. But he was given no time to recuperate. With a convulsive leap, Dirshan straddled his body. Pinning the man's arms to his side with his legs, Dirshan seized the man's ears, and using them as a handle, bounced the man's head against the ground. While the man's helm was obviously padded, it was not meant to take such punishment, and Dirshan was rewarded by the limp body beneath him. He was just getting up, the battle won, when the sharp clang of steel meeting steel came from behind. He turned quickly, only to see Heletaroy dismounted and holding his curved sword for another blow. The first man Dirshan had felled sprawled at his feet, a small dagger in his limp hand.

"Spawn of an imp!" Heletaroy said, even as he eyed the body. "But I think that he'll stay still for a while." Both men grinned at each other. No other words were necessary; there was no victory gained unless it was through risking one's life. They had the victory here.

Finding his legs a little unsteady—a common reaction after battle—Dirshan passed Heletaroy, clapping him on the shoulder as he passed in wordless camaraderie. He picked up his blade and wiped it on the jerkin of the dead tribesman—the one who had been killed by the man he had just stunned. Dirshan thought he could put a name to these men. Ayal. There had been the ruthlessness in their decision to kill the man which Dirshan had not seen before unless it was the truly committed—or in the desperate. He ripped the sleeve of the dead man, exposing the arm where the right shoulder muscles bunched to form a knot. There in deep blue was the tiny symbol of a bear. "He would have yielded," he said to Heletaroy. "I would not have had to kill him."

"I agree," Heletaroy murmured. "You offered him honor. And it seems that this one"—he indicated the sprawled body by his feet, whose form his eyes never left—"understands the speech. I have seen the like of these two before. Know you aught of where they come from?"

"No, only by report. They are of the Ayal."

"Yes, I fear that you are right. But I have seen them before, and I need no identification besides this"—and he used the point of his blade to disturb the necklace of bones that encircled the prone man's throat. "Knucklebones, and they are from men." He spat. "I had one put to the question not long ago—the only one we took alive. He said each bone meant another man devoured. He also had the blue tattoos. I had him buried alive after he managed to bite out his tongue."

"Did you manage to get any information?"

"Palcin is one much skilled in the extraction of tidbits, but that one spoke few words in the tongues of either plain or mountain. We could not read his writing after he bit his tongue, though he bled swiftly afterward. But if this one can talk, we shall see . . ." The sound of clattering hooves came from over the brow of the hill. It was Palcin, followed by five others in the forward troop. Blood was on all their garments, and all the weapons that were drawn had seen use. He saluted Heletaroy.

"Report!" Heletaroy ordered, after motioning that some of his men should dismount and bind the living captives.

"Sixteen wounded, five dead, four horses for us. The ambush was opened prematurely, at least from their point of view. Bahra circled around when he heard the horn and trapped many with their backs to the river below. They sought quarter. We now have them in a small clearing on the other side of the water. There were at least thirty dead for them, but I did not stop to count the bodies.

"I see that you have also been busy," Palcin continued, licking his lips in anticipation. "Are these two for me?" he asked. Dirshan did not like the animal reflected in those eyes.

"Yes, but do not question them until camp has been erected and patrols are out. We go no farther today. I want to know what is ahead. See to it." Palcin made no answer, but merely nodded in submission and then rode over to where one of the captives was standing, supported by one of his men's shoulders. He tore off the man's headgear, exposing the short hair, and knotted his hand in it to jerk the man's head back. He said something inaudible, but Dirshan saw the bound man stiffen. Dirshan turned his head away. He did not like torturers—even his own.

"Pity him and not the bound man," Heletaroy said softly. "On the last raid, they found his brother still roasting over the spit—they had eaten him piece by piece."

Dirshan did not reply. He rubbed his cramped muscles as he looked over the churned-up ground. Four lay dead there, and all seemed to be of his tribe. How many would have returned to Rema if given the chance? He would never know.

Shrugging, he walked over to where Heletaroy was mounting his horse. Another stood there, the reins dangling on the ground as it nosed for grass amidst the blood. It had been left by one of the troopers, apparently so that Dirshan would not have to walk down the hill. He mounted, bringing his face level to Heletaroy's. "Then you did believe me? About the Ayal? And you knew more?"

Heletaroy kicked his horse into motion as Dirshan rode beside him. "Of course! Do you think I would have come this far merely to fight a bandit?" And he laughed, kicking his horse into a trot down the hillside.

The road below was a milling mass of mounted troops, both those who had taken part in the skirmish and those who had come up as the horn had sounded warning. Here and there orders were already being shouted to make camp, and as they rode through the ranks, they could hear the excited buzz of conversation. The men on guard tonight would be very alert. They rode past the small ford, the shallow water not even reaching the hocks of their horses. One corpse, trapped in a deeper eddy of current, was floating in the water below it. The sightless eyes stared at them, blood seeping from the deadly head wound. But it said nothing as they trotted out of sight, victors on the field of the vanquished.

There was a small clearing on the farther side of the belt of trees which lined the creek. Many of Heletaroy's men were already busy setting up camp. A small knot of men waited dejectedly to one side, guarded by a group of mounted men. The two rode up to the group. Dirshan said to the Anshan commander, "Let me handle this, if you will permit?"

"You need ask after the fight above? Do as you will!" he snorted, cocking his eyebrow.

Dirshan looked over the men, counting twenty-one in the whole group. He assumed that some of the original party had escaped. All their weapons were in a pile on the other side of the clearing. All seemed to be Garazi.

"Clansmen," he said in his native speech. All looked up, most with sullen defiance. "How many are from the Bears?"

There was no answer. Then a slight shifting of positions toward one man to the side alerted Dirshan to their leader. He turned to face this one, pointing with his finger at him. "You. Do you claim the Bears?"

The man looked Dirshan over for a moment before speaking. "Aye!" he cried, ripping up his torn jerkin to expose the sign. "I and these follow Aliffa, as will all the clans to drive back these invaders from Anshan. Except those, of course, who have allied themselves with them. But then, they could not be of the clans." He hawked and spat, others watching him with granite eyes.

Dirshan rolled back his sleeve, showing the tiny hawk on his huge arm. "I am Dirshan, leader of the Hawks. I would kill you for your insolence, Bear, but not because I ride with those of Anshan. You and yours have defied the Shrine and now seek to link yourselves with the carrion eaters, the Ayal. What other choice does a man have, but to fight such?"

"They were there but to observe," the other responded hotly, though there were murmurs behind him. "Aliffa saw no harm, for they do not invade our lands as the Anshani have done. I would fight as warmly to keep them at bay, but in this I must obey my clan. It is the way."

"Yes, it is the way. But in this it is the wrong way, as you will soon know. Have you fought for the Order?"

The leader said nothing for a moment, then replied, "Who has not done so as an adult? I was west of Anshan once and followed the dictates of Shrine and Order. It was in the past. We now seek the old ways in which there is strength."

"Ways which the Order conquered once and would fain conquer again," Dirshan said simply. "But I do not seek to argue with you, for you think you have the right. Yet if one follows the way you seek, what happens to those captured?"

"Death!" the other spat out.

"And that of the Shrine is simple life to all who profess to follow the way. Then it would seem you have a choice. I assume that you answer for all here, but speak with yourselves about what I say. If you wish to follow the old way, I will oblige. I am of the clans, as many of you may have heard, and know what must be done. You will die at my hand, and your sign will not be defamed at that death, for it will be honorable.

"Yet should you chose to return to Rema, that is a price I will have none of you pay. You may take your weapons and leave, after your oath not to return to Aliffa. If you are caught forsworn . . . You know the punishment. You may bury your dead before you leave.

"But know well one thing. I have killed the great sow bear of the highlands: Hawk against Bear, new ways against the old. You may each see the teeth, claws, and skull before making your choice. The Hawk won, and so did the Shrine. Take it as a sign that the old ways have died. There is no quarter for those who fight beside the eaters-of-the-dead." He raised his voice. "I have said that they will be destroyed. If you accept these terms, then spread the word. We march on Aliffa and his allies, the Ayal. None who stand against us will be spared, for they are allied with darkness."

Dirshan reined his horse aside, and waited before riding toward the tents. "You have until dark to decide. The choice is yours. I hope I will not have to kill you all." The two men rode away toward the tents.

Then, while Heletaroy listened to the various reports, Dirshan checked on his motley crew. Ke'in had suffered no injury, though an arrow had taken his horse and thrown him in the process. Gett had killed two men, a report he made with some satisfaction, as they had rushed out of the ambush in an effort to take Iyali. Dirshan reserved his last comments for her, sitting apart on a stump. "I see the arrows did not find you," he stated. "A charmed life?"

"There is no weapon wielded by man which can harm me. There is no charm involved. The time of my passing was set cycles ago, neither to alter or change. That is not true for you, however. I am pleased that you have come out again; it seems you have a charmed life."

"It was foretold that I should know the time of my own passing, and I have not yet seen it." Dirshan laughed dryly. "But I, too, am happy I have not passed the Veil."

"The two captured Ayal—you expect information?"

"Yes. Heletaroy assures me that Palcin is most persuasive in freeing a tongue. We know one man speaks mine."

"Good. Then let me have the other. I have my own ways, and they are trained to resist. I do not think that your method will get much, whereas mine . . ." She let the comment trail, but Dirshan still remembered the night he had first met her.

"As you wish." He could question only one at a time. "If you are not successful, well, there is always the other way." He turned away, to find Heletaroy approaching.

"That was a masterful stroke with the clansman. Even now one comes with his weapons." He motioned with his hand at the advancing man now coming toward them, followed by two with spears from Heletaroy's command. It was the same man who had spoken with Dirshan afore. "I would see the sow's hide," he stated.

Dirshan motioned wordlessly to Ke'in, who was standing to one side watching. Without comment, Ke'in reached into the packs and removed claws, teeth, and skin of the head and dropped them all to the ground. The man walked over, toed them with his foot, and then bent to look closely at the brindled hair and torn ear on the skin. "I have seen this before—it is the sow. It was a good dream," he muttered, "but in my heart I knew it to be wrong. Word will be passed to all I meet. I never did trust this allying with the Ayal." He spat on the ground, then saluted Dirshan with the gesture of those who fought for the Shrine. "I fight for the Order again," he said and then walked toward the ford, to pass over to where he could begin to bury his dead. At his wave, the rest of the men who had been captive stirred forward, permitted to do so by a signal from Heletaroy to his men. One by one they filed past the tokens on the ground, then saluted Dirshan before going off to follow their leader. When the last man had filed past and was across the clearing, Heletaroy made one comment: "If the first one had not been satisfied, he would have fought, no?"

"Of course," Dirshan said.

"And you would have had to fight them all, one by one. Sooner or later, one slip . . . and, you pass the Veil."

"Perhaps," Dirshan answered, "but it did not happen."

"No, it did not." From that time forward, Heletaroy watched Dirshan with a new respect and deferred to his judgment.

IX

The scream pierced the late afternoon air. It came again, echoing across the clearing and the scattering of erected tents. The man had been screaming for an hour.

Sitting at the side of a small cook fire, Dirshan chewed on the leg of a roasted bird, the juice dripping down his chin and hands. He was not visibly disturbed by the screaming; it was a necessity without which he would not be able to get the needed information. But in one sense he could feel it; and like most of the men in camp, he wondered about the limits of his endurance under the fiery administrations of Palcin. He did not know.

Gett, who with Dirshan and Iyali made the third of their group around the fire, was not so reticent. "Think he'll find out anything useful?" he asked again, this time directed at Iyali. Dirshan had not answered him. "He shows some skill with the brand. There's not much left of the Ayal's feet." Gett had some interest in those matters and had gone over to look at the place where Palcin had erected a torture rack. His report back to the group had been informative. Dirshan now knew how Palcin would not let the Ayal cheat him as had the other. The scream was the kind of noise a man made with a stick lashed across his mouth to keep it open and prevent him biting his tongue. Dirshan realized that it would be very difficult to make a man talk with his mouth thus bound, but doubtless Palcin knew what to do. He had been fairly resourceful up till then, though Dirshan considered that it was no trick to cause pain. He himself had done so. What bothered him was that Palcin seemed to enjoy it; but then, it had not been Dirshan's brother which had been eaten by the Ayal.

"It seems crude," Iyali answered Gett's question. "Perhaps he will find out something. But the Ayal are trained to endure much pain; it is a form of offering to their gods. It is said that an entertainment at their firstborn feasts, where the 'flesh' is eaten, one of their torturers will exhibit his skill for the guests. There is a saying in their tongue: 'No sweeter sound than the racked captive.' Those prisoners who maintain silence are given a quick death and are not eaten.

"Yet it doesn't matter, I have found out what there was to know from the other." She had already had her talk with the other captive, who had been tied in the back of the tent assigned to Dirshan. There had been no screams from that session, but she was smiling when she returned to the fire. Gett had passed within to look, and had returned to Dirshan and given the universal signal for death: finger across the throat. Dirshan had made no comment except a nod, though he had again wished he had not come across this woman. He knew that she would tell him what she had found out in her own time and way. But he decided that he would not give her the satisfaction of asking, nor be forced by his own curiosity.

He threw the bone he had been chewing into the fire and wiped his hands on a piece of cloth. Then rising, his muscles complaining after a day of battle, he went over to Gett. "Here," he said, slipping the ancient dagger from its sheath. "Take this and kill that poor wretch that Palcin has. If he complains, tell him he is my captive, but I wish him dead."

Gett rose, about to speak, but then he looked at Dirshan's eyes. "As you command." He disappeared into the brush.

Dirshan reseated himself, taking up the other leg from the slaughtered fowl before him. He was halfway through it when another wrenching scream was suddenly cut short. There was the sound of argument in the background. A moment later, Gett came out of the brush. Wiping the blade on some leaves, he handed it back to his companion. Dirshan made only one comment, directed at Iyali. "I am not Ayal." He was still chewing when Palcin, followed closely by Heletaroy, broke through the brush to confront him.

"Why did you have him kill the man?" he demanded. "He would have spoken sooner or later. He was breaking already." His hand was on his sword and the blood pulsed rapidly in the distended veins of his face.

"Because," Dirshan said, watching his hands closely, "he would have told you nothing. Once you removed the stick and tried to make him talk, he would have bitten out his tongue. Men who know they are going to die do not respond to threats on their lives. He had suffered enough. His pain would bring back nothing, including your brother. Besides," he indicated Iyali to his left, smiling slightly, "she has found out what we wanted to know from the other. And," Dirshan paused, looking over to Heletaroy, "I do not like to eat and listen to screams in the background." He took another bite of food.

Heletaroy laid his hand on the shoulder of his second, and there was understanding in his eyes. "Go!" he ordered him. "Drink some of the wine in our tent. You have followed the Shrine for too long to try the customs of others."

Palcin said nothing for some time, his face working as he looked at Dirshan. Finally he sighed, a sound as loud as the wind in the trees. "Perhaps *you* are right," he said heavily. But from that time onward, he looked at Dirshan with hate in his eyes. Then he turned and walked away, but the set of his shoulders was straight and his head was unbowed.

Heletaroy joined them and took one of the wings of the bird. "His brother and he were alike in mind and body, born on the same night. He grieves heavily." He took a bite of the meat. "But you were right—that is not the way to avenge him. Even he knows that, I think.

"What did the other tell you?" he asked Iyali. He had been told that she knew the old ways of extracting information and had agreed to give her a chance.

Iyali was thus neatly boxed by Dirshan into telling what she knew without his asking. She smiled ruefully at the clansman. "Well done," she said as an aside, before answering Heletaroy.

"Not much that was not known before. The Ayal are indeed marching west, searching for their old lands to settle. These mountains first and then eastward. They have allied themselves with Aliffa, as we suspected. But already the mountains are ringing with a call to arms given by you, Dirshan. Already it is whispered that you have killed the great sow of the highlands. Some of the clans lean to you; others lean toward Aliffa. It was thought by that Ayal that this would mean difficulty, for they have put much effort into splitting the allegiance of the clans from both Order and their traditional loyalties. That you are a threat is certain, and they decided to act before you came farther.

"Small groups—such as the one today—were sent south as raiders and scouting parties. Their orders were to find what strength comes to you and if possible to ambush us. The main purpose was information. Yet it is still the Bear clan which does the fighting, not Ayal." She was silent.

Heletaroy mulled this over for a moment, then asked, "How many do the Ayal have under arms and marching? Where is their main camp, and how far from the hold of Aliffa? Will they help their ally?" Plain on his mind was the thought of a strongly reinforced army which would easily capture or destroy both his and whatever force Dirshan could muster.

"He was unclear on all these things when I asked—he had been apart from his war band for over a month. That camp had been a tenday on the road from Cascalon; though, of course, it is certain that it has been moved. If my knowledge of the eastern road does not run faulty, that would put the main body of the Ayal at least two tendays—perhaps even a moon—away from Aliffa's hold. That would be two tendays from here. We will reach there about the same time. In this I am not positive. I have not passed that way in some time." The way she said this made Dirshan wonder if it had been even within the last Great Cycle of the Worlde. "But that is what I understood.

"It is difficult to get any useful information out of an Ayal," she explained. "Especially one that speaks only his own tongue.

I speak it but imperfectly, and then I can understand only simple things. They have only one word, for example, in their tongue for stranger—but that word also means enemy, and it could be stretched to mean food animal. We do not think in those terms. It has been said that how we speak has much to do with the way we see the Worlde. I can assure you that the Ayal see the Worlde much differently than we do." Dirshan almost commented sourly that if anyone, Iyali saw the Worlde in much different terms than even the Ayal. But he didn't, in the interest of having peace in the camp.

"Did he say aught about men brought against us?" Heletaroy asked. "That would be most useful."

"I asked him three times in three different ways. All he knew was 'hands of hands of hands'—except for their priests, their concept of numbers is hazy. If the whole tribe of able-bodied males was on the march west there would not be less than twenty thousand, though some of those would be support and supply. Many of the Ayal serve apprenticeship in their religion, much as we do with the Order. At certain times—three days before a full moon, for example—they have an obligation to inflict pain. The vocal result is considered a hymn to their gods. Usually this is done with one of their food animals—a breed of men raised for food—but now they are on the march. I get the impression that they are hurried for some reason."

"Well," Dirshan said, "we'll get no more out of his mouth now. Why did you kill him? He might have been useful."

Iyali looked at him with a curious expression on her face. "I didn't kill him—he did it himself. The Ayal have strange customs. Before they go on raids, the men in the tribe have a spell put on them to kill themselves should they be forced to give information. By my means I only delayed what he would have done at his first opportunity—even if he had to throw himself on a sword by attacking one of us.

"As for the man Palcin was torturing, he was low-caste; otherwise he would not have known another tongue. The Ayal hold that only an animal can learn the tongue of another—that's everyone who is not Ayal—and so only those who have already transgressed some tribal law are put to such learning. You would have gotten nothing from him. They will bite out their tongues if they are tortured, and they are not taught to write in any language. Torturing him would only have satisfied Palcin, but would have gotten nothing useful."

"So!" Heletaroy said, spitting in disgust into the fire and listening for a while as it sizzled and popped. "All we know for certain is that somewhere to the east, perhaps already linked to Aliffa, is a force of large size ready to fall on our backs when we least expect it. Unfortunately, we already knew that, so the trouble you took to get two prisoners was wasted, Dirshan. Or maybe not so wasted. At least they do not know for sure how many men I bring with me. It may be they will retreat, fearing that there is a force much larger than our own. One can not fight without intelligence."

"That was a matter I forgot to mention," Iyali broke in. "There were two more Ayal with this raiding party. They left before battle was joined and thus escaped. I suspect that even now they ride hard to warn Aliffa and beyond. The Ayal did not prosper without caution."

"Aye," Dirshan joined in, "but I do not think that will matter so much. I do not fear the Ayal so much as I am interested in the doings of the clans. We have come at a time when the Ayal move west, but we were unexpected. Their worry will now be that we will serve as a rallying point, especially if we can get the clans to believe in this threat to their own lands. And that they surely will do once they learn that this is not merely a fight for the old ways.

"You saw for yourself the reaction of those who were captured this afternoon," he continued, addressing Heletaroy. "Aliffa may have the sworn allegiance of the Bears, and from those who have forsworn the Order. But—and as a clansman I know—that allegiance will not hold once it is clear that the Ayal are not simply allies. We have held these lands for many cycles. They are home to us, and we will fight to keep them. Every feud would be suspended.

"No, I think this advance of the Ayal is something in our

favor. Aliffa may like power, but even a bandit must have some-place as lair. Every foot the Ayal advance along the western road will drive another away from allegiance to Aliffa and back to clan and Order. I know my people."

Heletaroy looked him over in sober assessment, saying at last, "It is because I believe you that we go forward in the morning. I now see the wisdom in releasing those who fought us this af-ternoon, though the men grumble at it. Even now they spread the word. It would be even better if we have no fighting and a return to Anshan in bloodless glory. I bleed easily." He laughed, making a strange sound in the stillness.

"But to more practical matters. I consider that we have at least a day until we meet some of the men you have sum-moned. Yet we are still invaders. Even though we travel with the best intentions, you have noticed that every hold we pass is empty. Do you have any suggestions that will prevent a fight with our yet-to-be-known allies? There is nothing more painful than dying on the spear of a friend. My concubines would hardly understand, not to mention the look of surprised stupid-ity that I myself would wear as I passed the Veil."

"I have already seen to it," Dirshan told him. "Ke'in left east before we pitched camp, with word of our coming and the skir-mish we had today. I anticipated some trouble, but he is known and will pass the word. Also, I gave orders that the hills on the other side of the Smoking Water are to be scouted, to prevent any more trouble like today's. Those of my clan he meets will see to it."

"Good," Heletaroy said as he rose to his feet. "Then I will retire to my tent and a bath. I have earned both rest and a clean body. Hopefully Palcin will have drowned his anger in the wine I left—it contains a drug which causes sleep and for-getfulness. He needs it. Until the morn." He saluted, then turned away to disappear in the gathering dusk.

Gett, who throughout the conversation had been listening intently but contributing nothing, shrugged and rose to seek his furs. "I don't worry, Dirshan. I've trusted you this far, and since you have a healthy respect for your own hide, I can do no more than stick close enough to you so that you'll also watch after mine. But I do confess that I wish we were both in some stew back in Alithar. At least there it would be warm." He did not like cold. Giving a mock salute to Iyali, whom he seemed to have accepted without demur in the last week, he went to his tent. The hide flap dropped scratchily behind him.

Dirshan sat quiet, as if the flames before him held secrets and he would abstract them by force of will. From far away came the muted voices of two sentries calling, and the minute peep of some lost frog which had not yet sought the warmth and safety of a bed of mud for the winter. It was a lonely sound amidst the quiet bubbling of the stream.

Dirshan took out the torque, which had till that time been secreted in his pouch. He held it up before Iyali. It gleamed coldly in the flames, two smudges plain on its surface where he had touched it. "Of what use is this thing?" he asked her. "Only the lost symbol of a dead and ancient king. Why should it not be melted into useful metal? A good sword is more use."

Iyali looked at it and then to him, her face drawn and cold even in the glow of the fire. "You should not melt it for the same reasons you have not done the like with the dagger at your side. It will have its uses, even though you do not know them now. Just by keeping it you will prevent the Ayal from using it, and that is important. They are as aware as I was that this is a critical time for them. Though I did not say it, this move west was made in desperation—either that or wait until the Order came for them. It does not take perception to know that now that the war between Empire and League is finished, the Order will again march east. Already they have felt some of this pressure, and it is certain that the Order would have fallen on them. They seek to prevent their own destruction. In that they are but human."

Dirshan held the torque in his hands, its faint coldness drawing warmth from his hands. "I left the Order many cycles ago because I saw no purpose in this expansion, especially by the sword. I think that one way of looking at the Worlde, as long as it does not conflict with what others hold, is as good as another. Intricate philosophy—the ability to convince oneself that whatever one wants to do is justified by what a god says through the mouth of a priest—never did interest me. I have known two Grandmasters of the Order, both the late and the new, and both were men of the Worlde without philosophical blindness. They did what they did because it seemed for the good of all, whereas I think that simply leaving others alone is blessing enough."

"Yet you are here," Iyali replied, "and in that passing you will do what is in the best interests of the Order. And I think you misread that purpose, for it is to keep fighting in check that it exists, putting it directly on barbarians rather than destroying their own homes. Yet does not your presence here indicate that the purposes are akin? Two forces which achieve the same purpose would seem to be alike: you are, after all, known in the Order as the 'God-killer'!"

Dirshan seemed to hear mockery. "Even though I have been banned from the Shrine for ten cycles? That does not seem identical to me. I came here because I had to avenge both brother and father. In order to do this, it seems that I must also advance the cause of the Order. But in this I sometimes have the feeling that I am being manipulated into action which I did not choose. I have felt so since meeting you. I have not questioned your presence here, nor the fact that Gett nor Ke'in has said naught of it. But I suspect you, and that because you have not told me all you know."

He tapped his finger on the torque, then rewrapped it in its scrap of skin to return it back to the pouch. "Of all those in this camp, yours is the only purpose I know nothing of. I have had much business with wizards, and more than one witch in my time. I call at least one my friend. Yet I do not have dealings with others unless necessary. You have traveled far with the intention of watching a war, which I suspect many would ignore simply because of battle. You are a woman."

Iyali smiled at him, the first genuine smile Dirshan could remember her giving him. "I am that, aye, though to judge by what you refuse, I could be an Ayal! Ah, Dirshan, could you but know it, you are one of those who alter the destiny of the Worlde, as I have also been one. I know something of your past. You refused to command the Order, knowing that it would have been yours for the taking. Through the Family, who would have followed your lead willingly, you could have ruled the Empire—perhaps even destroying the Kalinthian Horde and retaking what weakness lost so many cycles ago. Instead you are here, again fighting to serve what you deem to be the right. Granted, you fight to keep the freedom of clan and kin, but that alone should not have called you from the ease and comfort of the Pillars in Alithar. I sometimes think the Order is correct and that we are in the grip of a larger plan, each step only preparation for the next. It has been so with me, so I think it shall be so for you. In this I cannot foretell, for my time draws to an end; and as I told you the future is clouded, the knot centering not far from here. Yet we still have the mastery of our own lives, to shape as we will." She rose, another smile on her handsome face. "I go to my furs. On the morn."

She was gone.

Dirshan stared into the fire for some time before he realized that he was alone. The snapping of some still-green sticks in the embers finally brought him away from his thoughts. He rose for his own furs, the darkness pressing in and concealing he knew not what. His would be a dream-filled sleep.

X

Dirshan was up at dawn; the small hours had been spent in restless sleep. He and Heletaroy shared a breakfast of cold meat, washed down by a thin and bitter wine; both watching as a strong force of scouts under Palcin left for the forward trail. Heletaroy wanted no repetition of the events of the day before, and, as he privately told Dirshan, "It is better to let Palcin think out this thing while doing something useful. He harbors a grudge against you, despite the fact that he is fully aware that you are right. There are times when action does more for a man than thought." Dirshan almost wished that he were one of the scouts for the same reason. But he was aware that Heletaroy wanted him close for an understandable reason—any trouble with the clansmen would be averted only if Dirshan was there. Otherwise the Anshani would be attacked as the interlopers they appeared to be.

They were already mounted and ready to ride when Gett finally came out of his tent, still rubbing the sleep from his eyes. Dirshan ordered him to accompany Iyali and follow in the second troop, not bothering to answer the resentful glance. Dirshan wanted no disturbing questions to trouble his mind on the ride, nor the even more troubling answers he was sure to get from Iyali. From this time forward, there would only be time to command and fight, something he felt competent to do himself without the dubious information of a sorceress.

The sun was midway to its highest reach in the sky when the lead party, Dirshan and Heletaroy in the van, finally broke through the encircling hills which had marched beside their road. A long grassy slope led downward to a wide vale; from above there could be seen isolated steads which dotted the fields, and here and there was a flock of grazing animals. A river traced a meandering path to and fro across the wide valley floor below. There was a faint trace of dampness which wafted up even to their place high above. A short time before, one scout had reported that the road into the valley was empty, but they would need no one to tell them that. The gradual slopes offered no place for concealment. They could easily mark the spot where the road turned north to follow the vale into the mountains; it ran roughly along the course of the river. Dirshan pulled up his horse—a new one since his had been killed the day before, and motioned below with his arm.

"The Vale of the Smoking River." He swept it with his hand. "Here is the center of the clans. Some consider it to be the one place where all my people are at home. The river is too wide and deep here to ford, though there is some raft traffic in the summer to bring lumber down to the steads farther south. The river does not freeze here, even twenty leagues north, where it breaks from the cavern under the last glacier. So cold is it there that the water will burn your throat. But it is warmer here. The grass stays green here and farther south for much of the winter, especially on the southern slopes. But we must follow the road north." He pointed.

"I have heard of this vale," Heletaroy stated, "at the fair—in conversation with some of your clansmen in a happier day. Happy is the man who returns to his home unscathed. War would do ill here; the land is too open. But it is good ground for horses and raising them."

"Yes, here and farther south are where most of the flocks are taken for winter pasture—here and in the far vales leading down to the river. But I came to take war away from here, and I am not unscathed."

"Where away does the road trend north? No ford?"

"Not here. Farther up, perhaps ten leagues, the water loses the force it gained coming down from the mountains and flows widely over a layer of hard stone covered with gravel. It is passable most of the time, though when the snow leaves the heights, one has to wait until the water recedes. It is here that the main meeting of my people is held in the summer. It is just as well that we have come now, for I do not like the thought of rafting men and horses across."

"I do not see much smoke, nor are the flocks as large as I would have thought if this is winter pasture," Heletaroy said.

Dirshan kicked his animal into a slow trot down the slope before answering him. "Most of the clans would have sent away everyone at the threat of war into the upper holds, which are more easily defended than the open land here. Only a few men and boys will be with the flocks, and they would not wander far in this lush grass. They are marked for ownership. Yet this is the season of retreat; the threat of clan feud or outside war only makes stronger what would already have taken place in the normal course of events. Even the bear sleeps in the winter, and here, in a sense, so does man."

They were a league out onto open ground, the troops which followed them strung out in columns of three, when the second troop broke from the gap behind them. The road was beginning its northward turning. For another two hours, they traveled on, the sun finally reaching its zenith. Men and animals sweated until they finally paused to rest and take some food. All along the road behind them they could see the massed men of Heletaroy's command, beads on a string the road tied together. Another scout rode up as they made ready to leave, reporting that the way ahead was clear. They traveled another three leagues before a hasty halt was called. Dirshan's sharp eyes had caught the hint of dust on the road ahead. Though it seemed to be only one horse, the speed at which it approached indicated a message of some importance. They waited until Palcin rode up, foam and lather dripping from the flanks of his hard-ridden animal. He gave a bare nod to Dirshan, though there was a demon in those eyes, before he spoke to Heletaroy.

"In another league," he panted, winded from the ride, "the road enters a belt of trees. All was quiet as I passed through heading north, but just beyond was a group of clansmen, all heavily armed and ahorse. They bade me turn back and go no farther. It was plain that they mean to bar the way. As I returned, I saw many filtering through the trees to either side of the road. They will fight us."

Heletaroy looked at Dirshan for comment, one eyebrow raised.

"If it were an ambush you would hardly have been allowed to pass to warn anyone," Dirshan said dryly. "I know the place you speak of—the moss oak. It is dense and brushy near the road. If they did not want you to see them, you would not have done so. This is my land. We have defended it before. I suppose it is a possibility that Ke'in did not get through, or that they are really only members of the Bear clan. But we must ride to find out."

"What exactly did they say to you?" Heletaroy questioned.

"Bid me return and tell my master that the borders of Anshan lie far to the west. That we should seek them, while we still have horse and body to do so."

"Well, Dirshan, it seems that your clansman did not get through, and no one knows exactly what we are doing here. What do we do now? I have no desire for battle."

Dirshan looked at him in silence; then, in answer, kicked his horse into motion. As he passed Heletaroy, he said, "I think we should go forward and find out exactly what they mean. Obviously they are not attacking yet. I would say that your men should stay here, and perhaps we can avoid any possible bloodshed." He rode on up the road. With a moment's hesitation, Heletaroy followed, after a curt "Keep them here until I return" to Palcin.

For some time the land had been changing, rolling more and more as the road followed the river and passed up the narrowing vale. The trees on the lower hills had become denser, and Heletaroy had noted that the road had seen heavy use in the recent past. Both men then topped a sudden rise and another vista opened up before them. Here Heletaroy caught his first glimpse of the wood Palcin had mentioned. The road dipped down into the backside of the hill, down into a steep valley. As was common, there was another stream hurrying down to the

river on their right. Yet on the other side the countryside did
not open up. Tall oaks overhung and shadowed the road, its
path a lighter tunnel in the dense growth. The belt of trees
formed a mass stretching right and left, and there was much
brush along the road.

Dirshan urged his horse down the trail with Heletaroy at his
stirrup until he came to the ford. There he paused for a moment, seeming to survey the woods twenty paces away. There
seemed to be no expression on his face that Heletaroy could
read, but there was a small tightening in his eyes, and his lips
pursed in thought. Then both rode forward.

The wood on the other side was cool and quiet. No sound of
bird or beast disturbed the silence. Heletaroy involuntarily
hunched his shoulders as they advanced under the tree canopy.
He could feel rather than see the unfriendly eyes who watched
and weighed them. They slowly clip-clopped forward, the road
rising again as they started to climb the farther slope and then
bent to the left. Everything in Heletaroy's experience told him
that he was about to die, and he began to curse his stupidity
for listening to this madman beside him, or, for that matter, for
having left the safety of the borders of Anshan. They came
around the bend.

Only to be faced there by five men, all on horseback and carrying naked weapons. Heletaroy had time in the moment that
they rode up to swiftly categorize them. Two were old, one
with the gray hair and mien of the respected elder; another of
middle age; and the other two young, one barely out of his
teens. There were no bows evident—just spears and swords—
but Heletaroy would have bet a stack of the Tors of far-off Sart
that there was more than one arrow aimed at his back. He
resisted the urge to unsheathe his own weapon, knowing that it
might be interpreted as a sign for a battle.

Dirshan reined in his animal about five paces from the group
of men, his hands resting easily on the saddle. Then he waited
silently, staring at the group before him.

The grizzled elder spoke first. "Your scout was told to turn back. Return to Anshan, renegade, and take your invaders with you." There was contempt in his voice.

"Before you are driven away with blows!" added the middle-aged one, his hand whitening on the hilt of his sword.

Dirshan said nothing to this for a moment, then drew back his sleeve to expose the tiny blue hawk tattooed there. "I am Dirshan, son of Eshca and brother of Shaget, he who was killed in the mountains by the sow bear. It was told to me that my father was taken and killed, and my brother's sons were not old enough to take their place. I seek revenge, both for my house and for my clan. Who seeks to bar me?"

The old man went to speak first, only to be stopped by the rapid speech of the second man as he broke in. "We know who you claim to be. Your sneaking spy came into the camp yesterday even as we prepared to rid the land of you. I am Levessu, of the Snake, which my father heads. It has already been decided that you are to be turned back. We need no help nor the aid of a turncoat; aye, one who even leads others to the invasion of his own land! Go! and before—"

His violent speech was interrupted by Dirshan's sudden spurring of his horse, the animal darting forward to bring him within reach of the speaking man. Dirshan's hand suddenly darted out, backhanding the man known to Dirshan as Levessu across one cheek and knocking him from his horse to the ground. The animal shied away, almost knocking down another of the men and coming close to stepping on him. "I am leader of the Hawk," Dirshan thundered, "and need no permission as to how and where I will ride in my own land! Keep your tongue civil, lest I have you brought to the circle and teach you the manners your father did not!"

He backed his animal away from the group and fingered the hilt of his sword. "Does anyone else gainsay my right to be here? I am of the clans and have the right. Or does anyone here wish to have feud with me?" He looked at the oldest man, the first to have spoken.

That one looked at him calmly, then down at the man who lay sprawled in front of his horse. "Such even your father would have done and given this man the right to a hearing before the rest of the clan leaders. I am Bucha, of the Snow Leopards. If you are Dirshan—and I can see the lines of your father's face in your own—then I salute you. It has been many cycles since you were last in these mountains; long has been the time since you left your hold to follow the dictates of the Order. Much has changed, as it seems you are aware.

"Levessu!" he ordered, the man below him now coming erect and eyeing Dirshan, "you were too hasty. If you want to enter the circle, I will be witness that you have cause. But I think you will lose. Find your horse and return to the camp. It will be something you can speak of later."

The man addressed looked up to him and then over to Dirshan. There was murder written in his eyes, but he did as directed and went up the road where his horse had stopped and was calmly picking at some leaves. He mounted and without a backward glance trotted up the road and around the next bend.

"Aye, Dirshan," the old one continued. "Much has changed. Your father and three others taken and killed, including Seney, the leader of the Snow Leopards, and the rise of this new power in the east. There is bad blood through all the clans. Many want to declare feud with the Bears. The younger ones are attracted by a vision of the old ways in contrast to the Order. It has caused a split between young and old, and as the power of Aliffa rises, so does the attraction of peace and the Order wane. Yet I have cause to question you. At your very back ride what have been counted at at least a thousand men. Some say that you guide them to the destruction of your own home; others that you do battle with Aliffa alone. Ke'in was in the tents this morn, but the report of armed men speaks with greater authority than the voice of a stripling. The Hawk are only one of the clans, but it was voted that we should find out first what you do in these hills before you are permitted to go farther. I think you will see that as reasonable?"

"Of course," Dirshan replied. "I would expect no less. Yet I come bringing an ally, not to fight the massed clans for the possession of my own home. Yet it would also take time to tell all, and that only to four men. How many of the clan leaders are at the meeting place by the ford?"

Bucha smiled, revealing worn and gray teeth with several prominent gaps. "Four are there: Snow Leopard, Badger, Fox, and Snake. The rest"—he spread his hands—"remain in their holds waiting to see which way the wind blows, though most of them have members present to see what occurs. Aliffa, of course, keeps to his own hold. Feud was declared by not only your own Hawks but also by mine and others after he killed the leaders after truce. For reasons I think you know, not very many of the Bears now wander these hills alone."

"I am the son of my father," Dirshan averred, meaning that he had been raised in the mountain tradition.

"Good, and for that alone you have reason to be here. As for the mighty Heletaroy . . ." There must have been a look of astonishment on the latter's face, for Bucha swiftly added, "I have been at the fair thrice in the last five cycles. I recognize you. And his men, also—well, that is another matter. We do not lightly suffer trespass on our ground."

Dirshan reached behind his saddle, removing a leather sack and handing it over to Bucha. The man looked inside. A smile creased his worn and lined face. "The head of the sow! Aie! Such had been reported, but it has to be seen. How long has this beast kept the northern holds at bay and served as a device for Aliffa's power!"

Two of the younger men with him started forward to look, one of them murmuring: "It is the skin! I myself saw the stripped ear when she took a sheep from my uncle's hold, two cycles ago. The Fox clan applauds this death, and the slayer!" He saluted Dirshan, his hand raised in the air.

"Take this to the meeting place of the clans," Dirshan said. "I ask only that I be given the chance to say my words. I will have Heletaroy encamp on the other side of the moss oak until I have had my say. This token should at least grant me leave to say my piece and a hearing before all."

"I guarantee it," Bucha said, this time with warmth in his

voice. "Return within a hand's passage of the falling sun, alone. We shall be ready to hear what you have to say."

Dirshan said no more, twitching his horse aside and riding away, with Heletaroy following. They rode slowly back in the direction from which they came, the same air of present danger quivering around them. Just before turning the bend and heading down to the ford, Heletaroy looked behind them. The road was empty, except for sunlight playing on the ground.

Neither said a thing until they had crossed the water and were mounting the trail as it led over the crest of the next hill onto the plain. Heletaroy came level with Dirshan, who now slowed his horse so they could talk.

"We could have died back there," Heletaroy said in a conversational voice. "One tiny misword . . . I could feel humming arrows in our backs."

"I also, but when one is swimming in a lake, it does no good to stop midway wondering if it is all right to cross. I did expect this kind of challenge. After all, to any other eye, we are come as invaders, and it is logical to think that I am but the guide. Yet I think we have crossed the main bridge; now remain only the smaller streams."

"Nonetheless, I would not willingly ride in your shoes this night—not without help."

"I do not do it because I want to, but because it is what has to be done. It may be that I will wind up in the circle of judgment this night, in which case you will have a stiff fight back to your home. But we can but wait and see. I am hungry. A Tor says I can beat you to the first of your command?"

"Agreed," Heletaroy accepted and without waiting spurred his horse into a gallop.

He won by a head.

XI

Dirshan parted from the Anshani camp shortly after night had fallen. To avoid any trouble, Heletaroy had ordered all his men into camp; their tents and fires made a line that could be followed as far as the road could be traced by the eye. Dirshan had had to take care of several problems before leaving, the foremost of which was presented by Gett. His companion had been adamant about the thought of Dirshan going into the camp on the far side of the moss oak and that alone. Dirshan's arguments that these were his own people and that his own kinsmen would likely be there left Gett unconvinced. Finally Dirshan gave him a flat order to remain. The little man, hurt and confusion writ large on his face, had entered the tent and was seen no more. Iyali was an easier problem, for all he had to do was place in her protection the torque he had been carrying. She had taken it with the words: "Only to hold," and then stowed it under her robes. No other words passed between them.

Heletaroy had then taken an early meal with him, offering advice which both knew to be useless until they knew the situation in the other camp. Dirshan took such concern as evidence of the Anshani's commander's faith in him and was pleased. In the short time of their acquaintance, they had come to be comrades, boon companions almost of many cycles instead of a short tenday. Palcin had not appeared. Dirshan understood without asking that he had been sent back down the line of following troops to encamp them. It was well from his point of view. He did not trust the other man, especially since the night of the torture. It was all too often that men in battle became

worse than their enemies, justifying their actions on the
grounds that this was the only way to defeat them. It was
Dirshan's opinion that Palcin had already seen too much of
what was on the other side of the Veil and it had warped his
judgment. He was glad that it was Heletaroy's problem, one he
did not want to cope with when the final showdown came.

All watched as he slowly trotted up the road, the line of light
reflected on his chain-mail receding into blackness. Just at the
brow of the hill he turned, his sharp eyes picking out the still-
standing form of Iyali. Then she was gone, and he plunged
down into the blackness on the other side.

It was well that the road had been in use for many cycles; for
during the day, the sky had grown gray with cloud cover that
came in from the south and obscured the stars. The white road
still glimmered faintly in the darkness, but he was forced to
walk his horse. The forest before him was a darker blot that
covered the hill beyond, and he heard—rather than saw—the
ford. The bubbling sound of water over rock was a comforting
sound in the stillness. Horse and rider splashed across, entering
the dark tunnel of the wood.

As before, Dirshan had the feeling that he was watched.
There was a brooding silence from an area which should have
rustled and hummed with the night activity of woodland creatures. It seemed to press around him as the path began its steep
gradient upward to the brow of the next hill. As he crested it,
he shook his shoulders to relieve the tenseness gathering there.
There was no more unpleasant feeling than to know one's back
was watched and not to be able to do anything about it. That
the archers who he knew were waiting did not fire was a positive sign, but he took little comfort from it.

Dirshan had passed along this road many times before in the
days of his youth, and he was not surprised by the continuance
of the wood. The area around the moss oak had been allowed
to run wild for just the kind of protection it now offered—hiding for defenders and exposure for the attacker. Though it was
only about two leagues broad where the road cut through it, it
stretched over twenty leagues north into the highlands and all

the way down to the banks of the great river now meandering to the southeast. It was a natural and effective defense and had served so many times before.

Dirshan wondered as he passed through about the lack of challenge, for though men could be heard more than once as they moved, no voice rang out in question. He assumed that Bucha had arranged for one man to pass, but except for sound in this Stygian blackness under the great trees, there was no way to make sure he was the only one. Dirshan considered this to be an unnecessary risk; his father would never have allowed it. He knew that should he dismount, he could have crept the width of the woods without disturbing a single sentry. He regretted now that he had not done so; it might have proved a point to the waiting clan leaders.

The trees began to get thinner, opening up on the other side of the wood into glades and small fields where the forest had been cut back. The trace of the road was now evident as it snaked a path between them. Far ahead—perhaps two leagues —the bottom of the cloud cover was tinged and lit by white, a sign that there was some kind of large encampment with great fires. Dirshan did not need that to tell him where the men of his tribe were located; directly ahead at the end of this road was a ford which crossed the smoking water of the river. It was a traditional place of gathering.

Now free of the trees, Dirshan increased his speed, noting now the night speech of beast and bird. A silent whurr and squeak from his left told of a great hunting owl, perhaps one of the Great Whites from the high country come into the softer south to find prey. There was a struggling beat in the wings and it was gone—now high in some tree to rip and tear at this new meal. Dirshan wished it silent hunting and a good omen for his own journey.

He cleared the brow of the last small hillock before he saw another human, pausing for a moment before the last slope into the emplaced tents. One man sat mounted at the side of the road, but he gave no word or challenge to Dirshan's approach. Looking below, Dirshan saw one of the largest camps of his people he had ever seen: spread over a league in distance on the flats beside the river. Across the river he could see more fires. He wondered if it was merely the threat of an invader from Anshan which had led to this massing of men, or if some impending feud among the clans had at last brought them together. Riding down that last steep path to the ford, he knew that he would soon know the answers to this and many other questions, just as he needed no direction to where he would find the present heads of the clans. Like many things common to his people, the meeting would be ruled and guided by tradition.

Long ago, when his people had come to these mountains, they had found the ford before him, one of only two places to take horse or flocks across. There, hard by the western side of the running water, the hills came down in a long line of uncapped stone, their sides half-covered with soil, their naked tops of rock clawing for the stars. Here, where the river foamed and beat an endless tune against the rock, a hollow had been carved by some event, there creating a natural amphitheater. In the center of it had been placed by some craft a black and naked stone, rearing five times the height of a man. It had not been raised by Dirshan's people, for they had not this skill in earlier times; but the clan leaders had swiftly discovered that a man, standing in front of this monolith, could make his natural voice heard almost to the top of the encircling hill. Though the land had been empty, those who had gone before had left this as a monument to their greatness. The clans thus used it, but they had no knowledge of how it had come to be in this time and place. Dirshan now thought he could put a time and people to the rock and wondered to what service its ancient top had been put. It was not a cheering thought.

As he rode up to the hollow, he found a huge bonfire burning in the center before the stone. With its light as backdrop, Dirshan could see the ring of mounted guards before him. A narrow path had been left open. He threaded his way through it as murmurs came from either side. In some of those faces and voices, he caught the sound of approval; others held doubt.

Dismounting outside the ring of tumbled stone, now tumbled and black with moss that formed a ring from wall to girding wall, Dirshan paced firmly into the firelight. There he faced the traditional array of his people, gathered in solemn meeting for judgment.

The natural hollow itself was not large. In cycles past, it had been marked into ten divisions, each corresponding to one of the clans. A crude seat of stone—actually a rock—was placed at ground level in front of each of these divisions; rudely carved on each was the symbol of the various clans. In a meeting such as this, only actual clan leaders and the heads of families were permitted a place, for there was not enough room to sit all the adult members of a clan. Still maintaining the silence which was shared by the massed faces which watched him, Dirshan walked into the center and faced them all. There he stopped, slowly pivoting to see all the men who watched him there.

Only five of the clan seats were filled: Snow Leopard, Snake, Badger, Fox, and, to his surprise, Snow Owl. A sixth—the Hawk—had many men backed behind it though the seat—now Dirshan's by right—was empty. In the light, Dirshan could make out Ke'in, who signed to him with a motion of his fingers. The seats of the Bear, Wolf, Mink, and Golden Eagle —the last the clan of the priests—were empty, though men sat in the seats behind facing him and the fire. Dirshan told perhaps three hundred men there, and for a moment he felt a cold gust as if he had been shut outside a door. Still he remained silent.

"So, renegade!" a voice said. "You did dare to enter the hold of your people." It came from the Snake, and Dirshan knew that voice. It was Levessu. He faced it. "Were you not warned fully in the moss oak?" it asked mockingly.

Dirshan did not reply. He removed his mail shirt with one swift movement, the cool night air pricking his skin, the heat of the fire evident on his back. With a ripping motion, he tore his sword from its sheath and plunged it point-first into the ground before his form, his hand on the pommel. "I claim clan right and defend it with my body! I am the Hawk. Does the Snake gainsay my right to be here?"

There was a muted murmuring and discussion from the area behind the chair of the Snake. Then, with a snap of fingers and the command "Fight!" the leader of that clan gave an order. Rising behind him, clothed as simply as Dirshan, stood Levessu. There was a naked blade in his hand.

The code under which they would fight was the ancient one, handed down in misty time by the rememberers since the days the Garazi had entered the mountains. Dirshan had claimed clan right: the right to be heard by his peers in formal gathering, and it was issued in the form of a challenge. Anyone who gainsaid that right would have to take it from Dirshan by force, and that to the death. It was remembered by the tribal word-keepers that on a time more than one would be allowed to dispute the right to be heard. Then Dirshan would have to fight as many, in sequence, as wished to dispute his desire. That had not been seen in recent cycles, and Dirshan hoped the old custom would not be revived. He was only so quick. Eventually he would tire, and then be killed.

Retrieving his blade from the dirt, Dirshan backed off as Levessu advanced. He looked over his opponent carefully, to find a weakness before the man found his. Dirshan had the advantage in height—perhaps four inches over the shorter man. But Levessu had a greater girth of chest and wider shoulders. His sword, too, was longer, and Dirshan knew that this would offset his greater reach. He had always favored the short, two-foot anlace as his blade, depending more on its weight and the ability to retrieve it quickly and thrust again than upon the short, stabbing point to pierce the enemy's defense. That advantage would be canceled out, for neither bore a shield.

Levessu advanced on him with the stealthy gait of the fencer, balancing on the balls of his feet and using the blade he now carried as a probe to test Dirshan's defense. Dirshan immediately placed him as a thrust fighter, depending on the point of his longer weapon to skewer heart or lung. A series of feints was deflected by the edge of Dirshan's weapon, the harsh clang of steel reverberating through the air. There was a roar from the watching crowd as the men backed apart.

Dirshan circled to the left, forcing Levessu to leave his blind side exposed. The other man played the circling game well, though; probing with his longer weapon and keeping Dirshan well out of reach. Dirshan paid careful attention to the man's right foot—stamp! stamp! and then a slide to the right—and when he was sure the man had adopted a pattern, screamed fiercely and charged in.

Loud was the sound of steel meeting steel, Dirshan timing his strokes to inflict maximum punishment on Levessu's sword arm, hoping to beat down his defense. Three short strokes were easily deflected by the man before him. Then Levessu suddenly reversed his wrist and ducked to avoid Dirshan's next stroke, coming in low off the ground with his blade. Dirshan was partially off balance and leaped on one foot to avoid the sweeping blade, coming down with his sword toward Levessu's head. He missed, but as his other foot found purchase, it landed on a small rock. Pitched to one knee, he had barely time enough to raise his blade above his head.

Dirshan's steel partially blocked Levessu's thrust, warding it away from his scalp and eyes. But it was only partially stopped. There was a sizzling line of pain as he felt it slide past one cheek, opening a shallow cut. "First blood!" screamed watchers from around the circle. Dirshan heard groans which he knew came from the Hawks.

Knowing instinctively that if he fell backward Levessu would spit him at leisure, Dirshan rolled forward, striking the outthrust leg of his opponent with his shoulder. Levessu pitched forward, his arm extended and body off balance, but he was well trained. Tucking his free arm underneath, he rolled forward and away, coming to his feet five paces from Dirshan. Both circled.

Now satisfied that he had accurately gauged the form of Levessu's attack, Dirshan allowed himself to be herded by the heavier man, waiting for an opening. Back, back the whirling blade drove him, past the edge of the fire and close to the black rock which rose dimly behind him. Levessu, becoming over-confident, lunged forward. The point of his weapon whickered past where Dirshan should have been, as Dirshan slid to one side. One short, chopping arc, and the fire glittered on Dir-shan's blade as it came down. He had intended to drive Levessu's weapon from his hand, but misjudged his cut and the forward momentum of Levessu's thrust. There was a bright gout of blood as the blade bit into Levessu's hand, cutting through to the sword right behind the looping guard. The weapon and Levessu's severed fingers fell into the dust.

Dirshan backed off, the cheers of the men around him loud in the air. Yet Levessu was not finished. Perhaps it was the bat-tle madness which possessed him or sheer hate for his oppo-nent because of the earlier insult. He bent, and then disregard-ing the slippery handle of his own sword, he grabbed it up with his left hand and faced Dirshan. There was reckless death in his eyes.

Dirshan backed off, watching him warily. It was plain to him that if the bleeding was not stopped, Levessu would soon die. The flow of gore from his hand was a red and black stream in the firelight. Yet Dirshan could see from the man's own gaze that he had disregarded his wound and was in the state which would make him take his tormentor beyond the Veil with him, in spite of his own cost. He aimed several slashes and cuts at Dirshan, two of which almost slipped past and gutted him.

The screams and chants around them were like a fly's buzz-ing to Dirshan's ear, but they were a small distraction. Another lunge by Levessu put Dirshan's back to the pillar behind them, its broadness preventing him from slipping to right or left. With a wild look on his features, Levessu ducked low and brought his weapon in, aiming directly for Dirshan's heart. He would plainly have sacrificed his own life to kill the larger man.

Though he could easily have done so, Dirshan did not want to kill the other man. It would only create more bad blood be-tween clans and aggravate what was already a bad situation, thus preventing him from gaining his main objective. He stroked his blade downward, aiming at Levessu's head. As he anticipated, his opponent could not help from twisting aside at least partially; not even the mad face death with calmness. He jerked his head and body to the left, though his point did not waver in aim on Dirshan's naked chest.

Still that was enough. Jerking his body to the right and bringing his blade across, Dirshan felt the other man's weapon slide past his ribs, the point slamming into the pillar behind him. In that instant, Levessu's blade was partially bowed from the force of his body pressing the blade into unmoving rock. Dirshan brought his heavy sword down on the place of greatest curve. There was the piercing sound of breaking metal as it snapped, pitching Levessu forward and into Dirshan. Quick as the hawk from which his clan claimed descent Dirshan slammed the hilt of his weapon into Levessu's head. Stunned, the man pitched forward into a heap at his feet.

A ragged roar of acclaim went up around the circle. Dirshan walked over to a spot in front of the Snake clan and stood directly before the clan leader, a man he did not know. Plunging his blade anew into the dirt, he proclaimed: "O see that I have claimed and won clan right! Does anyone now seek to bar me?" He looked from face to face in the crowd, which had now gone silent, finally staring at the clan leader before him. The man stared back with brooding; then his face lifted into a weak smile of rueful welcome. Rising from his stone seat, he walked over to Dirshan, clapping him around the shoulder.

"Welcome, Hawk, son of a worthy father. Long have you been away from the land of your people. None here will seek to bar your speech, and I will defend it with my body back-to-back beside you." This time the cheering was nearly unanimous. For the first time since he had left the camp of the Anshani, Dirshan felt that he might see the new morrow.

With curt words, Caritim, the leader of the Snake clan, ordered those of his people to tend the wounds of Levessu. As the man was carried moaning from the firelit circle, he briefly introduced the other clan leaders present. Dirshan robed himself anew in his mail shirt and took the high seat of the Hawk, facing the fire and the other men who now recognized this as his right. There was one shout from the men behind him, led by Ke'in, and they lapsed into silence. Then into the firelight strode Bucha, spokesman for the Snow Leopards.

In brief words he summarized Dirshan's approach with the troops of Heletaroy, proving to Dirshan that many of the shadows which had followed them were not of the Bear clan. Most of the men in the circle were appraised of the major facts, but in meetings of this kind it was customary to start at the beginning so that the clan rememberers would be able to state all at some later time. Finally finished, he motioned to Dirshan. Having only then reached the high seat, Dirshan had had no time to appoint the usual spokesman for his clan, but he wanted to speak for himself. Rising, he went to the center before the pillar and began to declaim:

"Men of the clans! It has been over fifteen cycles since I last stood within this circle. At that time I pledged body and sword to service in the Order, leaving clan and tribe to enter the rule and forms of the Shrine. For the greater glory of Rema, so that if I passed the Veil I would do so knowing I had advanced the light some small step.

"This, I think, I have done. Yet in that absence I find that not only cycles have passed, but also the faith which had made the Garazi strong. Order forgotten, old gods brought from the dead past, and clan against clan; remnants of the dark days when all we fought for was grass and wood in some high dale. I have even come to find that clan leaders, among them my own father, were taken under flag of truce." At this his voice grew sad. "Now I think I find myself in a different land, with new customs, and my people are no more."

He paused for a moment, ignoring the whispers that rippled and caught among his listeners. "Have the clans so forgotten the old days that they believe that legends have come to life again? Are there men here who believe that the Snow Leopard or the Badger have taken on the shape of man and go forth, to lead up into greatness?" His voice was scornful and rang in the hollow. "How many here have fought for the Order and in so doing proved with their own bodies the truth of its words?"

He stopped again. Then here and there in the throng men rose to their feet, to be followed by others until almost the whole body of men was standing in silence. "I see," he said heavily. "Then there are some who still remember the recent past and the cause for which they fought, and some, kin to us all, have passed the Veil to protect." Men began to seat themselves again. Here and there were smiles of uncertain recognition and the remembrance of old days past. Dirshan motioned with his hand at the hide bag he recognized close to Bucha's foot. The man picked it up and tossed it to Dirshan. Dirshan reached in and pulled out the head skin of the sow bear, holding it aloft and making a circle so that at this time all could see it. He stopped in front of the Bear clan.

"Here, in my hands, is the skin of the sow that Aliffa claimed to be the god of the Bears. It is dead! I killed it to avenge my brother. Its carcass now feeds the wolves in the high valley—it was naught but a beast and is now food. I myself fed off this god, eating of it to give me strength. It was an animal— but we are men. I do not believe in gods that can be killed," he finished and threw the head into the dirt. There was a general shout from the men of the Hawk clan and sober looks from those in the high seats before him.

"Yet we have all known men who should be dead. This new bandit—this true renegade from the clans—who claims leadership of the Bear. That is a man who should die. And I say this not because of my father, for that is the duty of myself and my clan. It is in the interest of all here, including the Bears.

"Look you at this man, Aliffa. He denies Order, claiming a beast as the true god. He splits the clans, upsetting the traditional order and pulling all to his standard to fight for what he claims are old clan rights. Yet it seems that this serves only to make *his* power the greater, while the clans fight for him and not for their own rights.

"Finally, there is this matter of the Ayal, the eaters-of-the-dead. I myself have seen two, captured with his men when they failed in an ambush. I know of what I speak. They are marching west. Who here will willingly serve up his clan to be their next meal?" Dirshan spat into the fire, disgust plain in the gesture.

"I think not one of us—even those of the Bear. I bring no war to my homeland with the troops at my side. True, they are of Anshan, and many of them are and remain members of the Order. Yet you have only to look, and many of you will recognize them as those who have fought at your side in the same cause and under the same banner. They have come, but at my request. And they have come to rid the Worlde of Aliffa, who is but a threat to the Order with his heedless attacks on its members and even to his own land with the destruction of our traditional ways.

"I, for one, will march east—if need be, alone, or with such of my clan as will follow. Those from Anshan come with me, to the same purpose. And, I think, any of the clans which still heed the Way and remember the insults which Aliffa has put upon us. And I"—his voice dropped in tone which carried in the hushed stillness—"will, for one, still see the Ayal stopped far in the east, before they are eating my own dead." Holding the sword aloft, light from the fire a flash which ran along the blade, he cried: "I pledge it, by my body and blade!"

The silence remained thick for a moment. Then, with a rush, the whole group of men sitting behind the clan marker of the Hawk rose to their feet, swords ringing and clashing as they were drawn from their sheaths. "By body and sword!" rang out the ancient cry, and then it came again and again as more and more men rose to their feet to do likewise—first as individuals, then in groups, as various clan leaders rose from their seats of power to do the same.

Dirshan looked around the crowded space, the echoes passing back and forth around the tiered space until there was drawn silence again. "I march tomorrow," he said quietly and walked out of the circle of flame into the darkness.

And it would be said by the rememberers in the cycles to follow that he had had tears on his face as he strode away.

XII

Much time had passed in that same night before Dirshan again rode south, this time escorted by Ke'in and several other family heads from the Hawk clans. After the emotional response in the meeting, he felt drained, but he had had to stay and have a planning session with the rest of the other clan leaders. Word had swiftly been sent that there would be war in the east, and messengers had ridden quickly to pull back the guards from the moss oak and allow passage to the ford for Heletaroy's men. At the entrance to the narrow tunnel into the trees, Dirshan dismissed his clansmen until the morrow. They would meet as soon as the rest of Heletaroy's men came up. He rode off alone through the now-moving trees, alive with the sounds of animals and birds, back to camp, not quite sure that the morn would not bring an attack after all.

Dirshan was challenged twice before reaching the first camp along the road, his passage barred by at least four of Heletaroy's men. Each time he gave the correct sign and was passed, a precaution he was glad he had taken before leaving. When he reined in before the commander's tent, it was to find both Heletaroy and Palcin, as well as Gett and Iyali, in the lit circle around the fire. They plainly planned to wait until dawn for his return.

"Greetings," he said on dismounting, signaling to Gett to remove saddle and arms from the animal's back. Feigning a strength he did not feel, he walked into the circle of light, accepting from Heletaroy the horn full of strong liquor the commander held out. "To our march on the East," he toasted and then drained the harsh liquor. It burned his throat; the finer vintages from Heletaroy's hoard had long since disappeared down thirsty throats.

"Then it went satisfactorily?" Heletaroy asked, knowing even as he said it that Dirshan's presence confirmed that fact. He knew he would not have to fight on the morn.

"Yes," Dirshan said and seated himself, hands out before the warmth. The small crusted scab on the side of his cheek drew the Anshani's attention, causing him to purse his lips, but he said nothing as Dirshan continued. "We have a meeting in the morning with those clan leaders who are present. Your men can advance to the ford; the way will not be held against them. Together we march on Aliffa. The clans have agreed to unseat him from his hold and cleave to Rema. He has been declared outlaw and the Bears absolved from their allegiance."

"Ah, good," Heletaroy breathed. "I had no relish for a fighting retreat—not in these hills, nor with men I respect. Heard they aught of the Ayal? I worry about those carrion eaters. They are just as liable to show at our backs."

"They knew nothing more than we already did from Iyali's questioning. But scouts had already gone out from my clan, and others leave tonight. We shall have word. Right now I need sleep. I have had a hard night, with some fighting." He tilted his head slightly, catching the light on the marked side of his face. "I had to prove clan rights," he added.

"The one you knocked from his horse?" Heletaroy asked.

"Yes, but if not him, it would have been someone else. It is the way of the clans, and I have been too long away. They would not follow anyone who does not show mastery of sword as well as mind. I think I showed them both, and they agreed to follow me in order to be rid of Aliffa.

"As for the Ayal, they are to them as you—the second of their worries at the moment. But my father used to say that one crosses the chasms as they appear, not before. It was good advice." His shoulders slumped, the tension draining from them. He rose, motioning to Iyali to precede him into his tent. "I will see you on the dawning." With nothing further, he passed into the tent, Iyali already within.

Within, she prepared to disrobe, only to be curtly motioned with his hands to stop. "I do not wish to use you," he said harshly. "Only I need information. I want to know fully what your purpose is in this camp, and what it is about this bauble of gold that makes it so important to the Ayal. I am tired of groping in the dark. I think you know more than you say."

"There is nothing more I can tell you. Just as I said, it is a meeting to which you are appointed, and I must also be there. I clearly saw both of us present at some final end, and at that point the vision cut off." Her voice was calm.

"It is my belief," Dirshan persisted, his voice low and dangerous, "that if Rema wanted men to see the future, all would be able to do so. For this power I distrust you, for I think you have looked on things no man should see. But I have sworn on sword and body to unseat Aliffa from his hold, though at the same time I think I have been manipulated into forcing an issue with the Ayal and this by you. I have no evidence that they intend a march west, except from your mouth." While talking, he had paced the floor. Then, with a sudden, sweeping motion he snatched her hair, drawing Akamatoth and holding the bitter edge against her throat. "I know not if you can die, or if weapon held by mortal men can overcome your powers. But this blade has taken more lives than live now within this camp—and not only by me. If this threat does not encourage you to talk, think on this: I will swear not to take part in any battle with the Ayal unless I know more, and I will know it before much longer."

Iyali made a strangling noise, trying to speak through his hand, which was clamped on her throat lest she loose some spell on him. He loosened his hand sufficiently so she could draw air. "Arrrgh!" she moaned. "You would be a rough suitor! And you are right. I think yon blade would kill me. Ever were I and those of my sisterhood at war with its users. I swear to tell you the truth as I know it, if you will but listen."

Dirshan relaxed his grip on her throat, but kept the point of the blade firmly against her throat. "Speak!"

"All of what I have said to you so far is true, except that I have not been alone in my foresight. I am an adept of the Tural; know you aught of what that means?" Dirshan shook his head. "We have concerned ourselves for many cycles with the growth of the Worlde, before the Order was on land or e'er the Shrine was built, when even the great strait had not been opened between the Heclos and Vinderclos. Aye, even when this blade was first used by a man to send someone to a forbidden god. I have not such great age, though I have seen and studied much upon the Worlde for many cycles. We try to help and aid the growth of what we see as good, aiding with what powers we possess to prevent the return of what was once conquered from returning to plague a Worlde which has forgot them.

"Nigh on a Great Cycle ago, when the Ayal were still present in these hills, there came a time when it was recognized that they must be ended, for the good of all. My sisterhood had some hand in this and myself especially, for it was my task. With our aid, men, some of them even your ancestors, came out of the south and drove the Ayal away. Their sorcerer-king was he whom you found in his bed of ice so far below the mountain. His power was indeed great, and even the greatest adepts could not destroy him; but he was driven into what was hoped eternal sleep—a sleep as deep as the roots of the mountain tomb they built to hold him. He left instructions with his own on how to bury what remained. Much of the lore which made them powerful sleeps with him and so they were driven away."

Dirshan snorted unbelievingly. "There was nothing in that cave but corpses—dead and frozen one cannot know how many cycles. But they were dead . . ." he added with conviction, trying to forget the vision of eyes which seemed to watch him even as he had removed the torque from the frozen flesh.

"If a frog is dug up from the mud in midwinter, it, too, seems to be dead. Put close to the fire . . . ah, then one sees the difference. So, too, does Cleyungit sleep, waiting for the right words to awaken him," Iyali answered him.

"Two things are necessary for that to happen. A gateway or

path has to be opened." She slapped a hand on the furs beneath her robe. "There is a lack of words to explain, but this does not happen frequently. Such a time is now approaching; it is the knot in time I mentioned. Through that time no one can foretell the threads or outcome. Then there must be present someone who can awaken the sleeper, with the knowledge of how to do so. Yet in their lore the Ayal have not forgotten it, and the time fast approaches. Hence they are on the march, and they seek to fulfill the old prophecy.

"As for the torque which you removed, it is a charm of old about which I know few things. By its use Cleyungit was able to control weather, to call down the biting cold from the mountains to sow death among their enemies—even to freeze a man in his path. Some of those spells the priests of the Ayal had retained, though without the torque they are useless. It contains the force which Cleyungit used to construct it and contains much of his power. But it is known that it will not work for a woman. There is some force which it channels that can not be focused by a woman; otherwise I would have taken it from you and done what must be done. So it was vital that you take me with you.

"I would have told you this when the time came for you to use the knowledge," she said finally. "Your part in this was foreseen, but beyond that all grows dark. Someone had to be on the spot, and I was the one chosen." She was silent.

Dirshan looked into her eyes for a moment, head deep in thought. What she said had the ring of truth, but he had the feeling that he had not extorted it from her in fear. Some other terror motivated her, though he knew not what. But he was satisfied for the moment; what she had told him made sense according to what he already knew. For a moment he wistfully wished for the services and aid of Handlig, called by the name of Artificier, who was a wizard of his acquaintance. But he was far away, in the dreaming city of Tyama far to the north across the wide Heclos. Shrugging, he kept his thoughts to himself as he sheathed his blade, then released her to remove his jerkin. "I'll sleep now," he told her. As she watched, he rolled into his pallet of furs, his back to the tiny lamp on the ridgepole. Iyali gazed at his broad back for a moment, a flash of irritation on her face. Then she removed her own robe and retired to her own furs. The sound of his whispered breathing passed in the darkened tent as she lay there in the blackness, many thoughts of cycles past eddying through her mind.

Dirshan rose to the muted sounds of Gett, stamping and thrashing as he tried to saddle the horses outside in the chill morn air. Iyali had already left the tent. As he came out, he found her before the fire, tending to the stew which was bubbling there. He nodded to her without comment, then spoke with Gett as his companion came up to take some breakfast. "I want you to ride with me back into my clansmen's camp, but speak to me only in the tongue of League or Empire. When I am in conference, I want you to mingle around as if you gawk at the wonders of Alithar, but listen closely. I wish to know what my people really think of this, not what they tell me. Understood?"

With a smile on his face for the first time in a tenday, Gett nodded his approval. "Aye, mate, a clever idea. And I was getting tired of playing guard for yon leman—she strikes me as capable of caring for herself. I was beginning to feel useless." He winked at Dirshan.

His spirits improved both by the conversation and the sleep which followed it before dawn, Dirshan returned the wink—age-old comment of man on the female. Any further conversation was precluded by the arrival of Heletaroy, who entered their campsite leading his horse. Tethering it to a small bush, on which it began to browse happily, he joined them. "I let Palcin handle the details of moving the men down to the ford. Messengers have already been sent to the men along the back trails. Are you ready? We have much to do."

Dirshan shook his head in agreement, his mouth full of stew. All three men mounted. In accordance with her role as leman, Dirshan gave Iyali orders before leaving to remain with the first elements of Heletaroy's troops, and that in curt terms. He was gratified by the look of sour displeasure that crossed her face, but she said nothing as she turned away and bent to her tasks. He found it hard not to take satisfaction from it, but it was small payment for her leading him into unknown danger. He did not like to play the fool.

The three set off down the road, Dirshan sitting in the middle so he could talk with Heletaroy, Gett on the other side watching the passing landscape. As Heletaroy listened, Dirshan gave him a somewhat fuller account of the previous night, then continued: "We are fortunate that we came just at this time and that those of my clansmen misread your advance. They had already gathered to contest your presence as well as decide what to do about Aliffa. There are no women in camp, for they are prepared for war. It could have gone either way, for his power, and even more important, influence, has grown great. Except for those he has deliberately offended, many would have chosen to fight on his side. It was not spoken, but I had the feeling that some gold has changed hands among the clans."

"It would not be the first time such has been used to loosen the bonds of friendship," Heletaroy said. "How many stand ready to march on the hold of this bandit?"

"Under arms in the various clans wait over three thousand; eight hundred of those follow me personally because I am from the Hawk clan. I think most of those will follow in our path, but some will stay on as a rearguard. I am afraid they don't quite trust either you or your men." He grinned. "I do not know the reason and can't understand why."

"Neither can I, but that is more than I expected. How many does Aliffa have under arms?"

"From those who have come back or even seen his hold, they say upwards of fifteen hundred are staunch to his banner. Many from the clans are disaffected, but there are not a few others from south, east, and north, brought in by the promise of loot and rapine. This may seem as though we have the winning of it by sheer numbers, but he is staunch in his hold and well provisioned. It is said to be a formidable place. We may have to stay and starve him out, but we are coming to the worst season of this cycle. And the Ayal are unpredictable. Should he choose to dispute the passes into the mountains with us, we would lose many. It was told to me that the land is pathless, with much opportunity for ambush and hidden assault.

"They have a map of the road leading to his hold in one of the tents by the ford. We shall see the shape and lie of it before we start out."

"Good. I am anxious to leave these hills. My men tire of this life in the saddle, as do I." They finished the rest of the ride in silence, galloping swiftly along the road. Once the formalities had been completed, only the four other clan leaders were present in the tent with Heletaroy and Dirshan. Before dismounting, Dirshan had pointed out to the Anshani leader the long file of men who were already breaking camp and crossing the shallow ford to the east, their forged links glinting as they moved in the morning sun. They left Gett outside, as if to watch the horses, and went in to talk with their new allies.

"Here," the leader of the Snow Owls had pointed down onto the map on the small table before them, "is the road as it leaves the ford here." He indicated a spot with his finger. "Three days' journey afoot, a day and a half ahorse. There is a side trail to the left here . . . and here, about three hours beyond that. Both come up and around by treacherous paths to the hold of Aliffa; one from the southwest, the other from the south. Both join into a single track shortly before his hold, thence up a rocky road to the knees of Muraaz. His hold is built within a cliff face there. One entrance lies at the end of a carven path up the sheer side of the precipice; there is another door at the mouth of a sloping tunnel that opens up beneath the hold itself. Both seem to be impossible to force if the men have enough food to keep themselves provisioned.

"Here, almost at the edge of this map, there is another faint road which comes in from the east. We have little knowledge of it, though his hold lies at the fringes of my own land." He spoke of land allotted to his clan. "The peaks of the range frown down and close off access from the south; it is a wilderness where not even the great goats of the mountains go. I know of it only because of a prisoner we captured—he tried to raid one of the isolated steads in the north and spoke of it. That this must be the way in which he enters and leaves his hold is evident, since we keep watch to the south and they do not use the paths I have already pointed out."

"There must be footpaths and trails other than these two coming in from the south," Dirshan said. "Perhaps men can be passed along them and prevent an ambush?"

"Possible," came the reply, "but if you want them moved at any pace faster than a snail, we must use the bigger trails. Already the cold is coming down from the lower hills. One scout has reported a storm on the lower road, and that usually does not happen for another two moons. There are few men from this area who are not already of Aliffa's hold and who thus know the land. Perhaps if we capture a few of those, we may be able to force them to reveal the trails."

"We shall see when we get to that point. How many days journey north until one comes to the hold itself?"

"Three, but it is hard riding and with much danger if the weather turns foul. There is no forage for horses nor anything to burn. Both must be carried. Word has already been passed."

"Also," added Nenten, clan leader of the Snow Leopards, "there is only one place wide enough before the hold which would allow many men to gather. It is here"—he showed the point and struck it several times—"but this parchment does not show the fact. Aliffa is cunning. His hold was built to keep men out. I see no way to take it."

Dirshan, who already had some ideas in that direction, though he wanted first to see the actual layout of the hold, waved it off with a shrug. "Hard worry, no nerve," he said in a quote from the mountains. They conversed some more about the order of their combined advance and finally decided that due to the composition of their forces, the Anshani would go up in a body down the first trail, which was the easiest, followed by the men from Dirshan's own clan. The others, all bred and born to the mountains, would follow up the second and more difficult because of their training and better horses. The meeting broke up at the approach of Heletaroy's first unit. They rode into camp to the cheers of some of the gathered clansmen. Heletaroy went to direct them onto the first leg of their journey east, across the ford; while Dirshan, after promising to join the rest of the clan leaders for a meal that night on the trail, went over to where Gett waited with the horses. Together they rode to the ford, watching as the first elements of Heletaroy's men splashed over as Dirshan listened to Gett.

"Most of what I heard was good; many seemed eager to be rid of what was a bad influence. There were a few mutters. Word has come of the activities of Heletaroy in the west, but whatever you said to them last night was effective. Many of them sing the glory and praise the wonder of the great Dirshan."

Dirshan gave Gett a quick sideways glance, but there was no evident mockery in his face. He let it pass, knowing that the smaller man would blandly deny it if he said anything. Dirshan was much pleased at this report. He had wondered whether, once the clear light of day had brightened up the emotional storm he had stirred the night before, many—perhaps most—of his people would be lukewarm in the cause. But it seemed his luck would hold. When Heletaroy rejoined them, they rode across the ford, joining the column which Iyali rode in, moving east along the main trail into the hills. It was a cold journey despite the bright sun.

The first two days passed swiftly. The Anshani, now joined by Dirshan's clansmen, made quick time along the main road, passing no one except an occasional scout going in the opposite direction. That they were being watched was evident; up on the brows of the high and rugged hills into the mountains that sought to enclose the road could be seen tiny figures of men on horseback. As the road led steadily east and then north, the weather began to grow colder, confirming the reports of their scouts. Snow lay on the slopes of the mountains to their left, and occasional eddies of some far-off storm swirled tiny, bitter flakes into their faces. Dirshan was troubled, as was Iyali. She plainly thought it to be the work of the hidden Ayal. They did not discuss it; they knew that it would only arouse fear in their companions.

Then they came to the turnoff into the first trail leading up toward Aliffa's hold, and it was here that the first determined resistance to their advance was felt. Iyali had been sent back to the third troop of horsemen—much to her displeasure, but at the insistence of Heletaroy—and so it was only Dirshan and Heletaroy, followed by Gett on the narrow trail, that the scout reported to. He stumbled back, his feet making shallow holes in the slowly drifting snow of late afternoon. "It's blocked," he cried on sighting them, then after regaining his breath, continued: "Looks like a recent rockfall—trails blocked like a stopper in a gourd. A rock came down just as I turned—broke my beast's leg. 'Twas a fine animal."

Leaving Gett and others who followed to tend to the evidently exhausted man Dirshan and Heletaroy rode forward. A half hour's ride upward, the trail took a wide turn around a massive hump of stone, part of the frowning masses around them. On the other side a long, sloping V-shaped valley was revealed whose one slope, that to the left, was pocked and marked with groups and pieces of boulders large and small. The trail wound along the bottom of this slope, but away at the far end both men could make out a giant plug which had been dumped, as if by some playful god, right across the trail. High and steep it reared, perhaps ten times the height of a man, and before it they could see the dead shape of the scout's horse, lying on its side with a huge boulder half-covering it. There was no movement on the slopes above, but Dirshan, after scanning the high crests, spoke quietly to Heletaroy. "There, high and to the left, there is movement. Likely a head, with arms ready to dump a few more of those bounding friends on anyone willing to try yonder slope."

"Yes, I saw it," Heletaroy affirmed after a moment. He looked away, concentrating his attention on the mass of immovable stone ahead. "It would seem that if one went carefully, skirting that one pile of rock where the red stone sits, that you could pick a path around that plug with some ease."

"Agreed," Dirshan said after some staring, "but there are those above us who will probably bounce a rock on our heads should we try. However, if they were gone . . ." He grinned.

"It does seem that we passed a tiny trail leading up and to the left a short while back," Heletaroy said musingly. "If several men were to enter that cleft, it would not be unlikely that one could come up and around those above and prevent this unkind bouncing of rock on men or beast."

"The subtlety of your thought astounds me," Dirshan said. "And I think I know three men to try it." They said no more, but turned their animals and rejoined forward elements of their troop.

Giving swift orders that the leading men were to wait for a count of five hundred and then press forward to the barricade of stone, they collected Gett and galloped back to where a faint trail led up into a cleft, then up and out of sight to the top of the ridge. Dismounting, all three men pressed forward on the narrow path, keeping low as they passed over the naked ridge of stone and then running wildly down the farther slope with Dirshan in the lead. Some scraggly thorn brakes grew here, and though bereft of leaf, they still provided cover for the advancing men. They broke through into the open, crawling from boulder to boulder on the reverse slope of the other ridge, trying to circle the others.

Dirshan's hand suddenly motioned them all to the ground. Indicating that the others remain, he laid his sword on the ground and crept silently up the slope toward a large rock. There, outlined against the sky, stood a watching man, waiting to give warning for precisely the kind of tactic the three were planning. But he was obviously expecting someone on horse— someone without the mountain skills Dirshan possessed. There was a soundless flash as the dagger blade caught the sun, a faint flurry of movement, and then Dirshan's head and hand appeared. Both Dirshan's companions moved forward. Gett picked up Dirshan's sword. When they reached his position, they flattened beside him, looking over the corroded slope beneath them.

Where they lay was a natural hollow in the rock; split-apart sections of rounded rock strewn here and there in a random pattern, some of them larger than a horse. This hollow was atop a knoll of native stone—the same knoll which overlooked the ridge line and then the long slope at the bottom of which the trail ran. A line of natural and emplaced boulders formed a bulwark on the top of the slope; under many boulders were long levers to push the rocks on anything that moved below. Crouched about these were ten men, all watching intently the ground below them. Their horses stood in a hollow below, one man guarding them. Far off, to the right in the valley proper, they could make out the threading line that was the first of their men coming around the bend.

Dirshan pushed them back soundlessly from the lip of the hollow, Gett scrambling to get away from the corpse which was the lookout, his throat now open without warning. "Gett," Dirshan hastily whispered, "you take the one with the horses. I don't care if they get away, but get him. He is probably there to warn those farther on about our approach. Go now. Strike when you hear the shouts of the others. I don't think you will be able to see anything." The tiny man grinned wolfishly and slid over the far side of the hollow, passing from rock to rock as he circled and made his way to where the man with the horses waited for his death.

"Left or right?" Dirshan asked with a raised eyebrow.

"The right. It's closer, and I cannot pass from rock to rock like a hill lizard. Shout when you're ready." Then he was gone, passing between two naked spires of stone as he made his way to the end of the line of men. Dirshan watched his progress for a moment, making a reservation to tell Heletaroy that he did much better than a rock lizard, before he picked out a path he would use to reach the farther man. Then he was up and over the lip of stone, crawling from shadow to shadow to the left of the unknowing men below.

The first man Dirshan killed was unsuspecting; his throat

was cut even as he yawned and shivered on his perch of stone. A large boulder shielded him from the sight of his fellows, and he died giving no warning. Creeping around the large boulder gave Dirshan a view of the entire line of men. It also told him that he would not be able to take another so easily. Knowing that surprise and boldness are the best substitute for numerical strength, Dirshan calmly gripped his sword and walked around the boulder. He was within three paces of the first man in the line before his neighbor on the other side turned, and, with a cry of horror, gave warning for his comrades' death.

Dirshan then knew that there was nothing to be gained by silence. With a roar, he cut through the spine of the second man even before he had a chance to turn. The third was still shouting as he futilely tugged at his sword when Dirshan caromed into him, knocking him off balance. That one he brained with the flat of his sword as he swept past, not even watching as the man fell heavily to the rocks behind him. Then there was the fourth in line; now turned into a group of howling men set upon from both ends, knowing not how many assailed them.

From that time to the end in silence, Dirshan was only aware of a sequence of sound and action. A shrill neighing sound came from below: the grunt of a gutted man who stumbled to death over the rim of the ridge. Another swore at an unknown god even as he stared at the severed stumps of both arms. From somewhere to the front, Dirshan heard the grunted battle cry of Heletaroy; he spun, parried, and then cut down the man who opposed him, breaking past to attack the next man in line who had already turned to flee. They met in the middle of the line, the last man already running down the slope and fleeing toward horses which were no longer there. His surprised grunt could be heard even by the two men above as Gett rose soundlessly from behind a rock where he had been hidden and decapitated him as he passed. His wave and shout said that no others had escaped.

"I see that you have again managed to cheat Rema of her due," Heletaroy said with heavy irony. "Such fortune for one so young, and often in danger."

"None greater than yourself. But I think that next time we let someone else do the work." And Dirshan pointed with his bloody sword to where the first of the line of men below were mounting the side of the rocky barricade.

"Agreed. Commanders should command and others fight." Heletaroy waved to the men below. "But come—our horses wait and I have had enough walking." They waited until Gett toiled up the slope and then passed over together. The first of Aliffa's obstacles had been passed successfully.

XIII

They stood before the hold of Aliffa.

A cleared space—really a hollow in the hills which here folded into a natural valley—provided a place where they could have an uninterrupted view of the massive structure looming above them. A cliff—flat-faced bare stone—reared its height over a furlong above, broken at midpoint by a hollow setback into the rock. Above that hollow the cliff continued straight up, jutting outward to overhang the valley below, appearing as if it would fall momentarily on the puny creatures who stood beneath it.

Into that one break in the cliff face Aliffa had caused his hold to be constructed. Slab-sided walls of masonry seemed to merge with the living rock, walling off what seemed to be a natural cavern of some size. A narrow space had been left between the risen walls and the top of the continuing cliff, wide enough so that a man could peer over; as indeed some were doing even as they looked at it. Stones would rain from that opening, as would spears, arrows, and hot oil. They gathered force with every foot dropped, crushing anything at the bottom.

A narrow path was carved into the rock. It wound to the left, thus exposing the unprotected side of any man careless enough to challenge the men who manned the walls above. That path terminated in a single door set into the stone, but this was wide enough to admit only one man at a time; Dirshan would have wagered that he would have had to stoop in order to enter. If he ever would, that is. And he knew that from its position that the door would not be forced.

Horses and goods entered through another portal, this one

much larger and placed at the base of the rearing cliff. Under cover of locked shields, Dirshan had examined this one. It was made of massive oak in two halves—barred, of course, from the inside. The whistling thud of falling stone warned him of what would happen should anyone attempt to force this. Even as they retreated, a stone fell, so heavy that it did not even bounce. It only crashed to a halt with a dull thud. No man there needed another to tell him that it would be almost impossible to force an entrance from the bottom. Dirshan himself would have backed the portal with a solid bank of stone and rubble. Since he assumed that Aliffa was no fool, he knew that it had also been done here.

Dirshan stood to one side in thought as Heletaroy and the rest of the clan chiefs quietly discussed how they would handle the looming fortress above. It had taken four days on the trail to reach this desolate spot high up in the range, one more than had been predicted. The weather had turned against them, bringing down heavy snow and a gnawing cold that seemed to feather its way beneath the furs the men wore and pierce the will of the strongest. Strangely enough, at least to the majority of their men, the snow and cold seemed only to follow the path of their march. Flanking scouts that Dirshan sent out reported that the slopes to either side were clear. Dirshan thought he could put a name to their misery and who caused it. His speculation about the Ayal was confirmed by Iyali: "They will use cold as a weapon," she had said, "for they have remembered some of the old spells." But they had toiled forward to a final meeting with those clansmen who had passed up the other trail to the spot before the hold.

Two more ambushes had been set for them on that trail: one the same type as the first, the second a series of barricades manned by archers high up in the forbidding cliffs. Both were forestalled by Dirshan's planning, for they had hit on the solution the first time. Fifty members of his own clan, dressed in winter white, had been sent ahead. Traveling afoot to either side of the main march, they had been able to come up behind the men who awaited them, either destroying them or giving warning. Dirshan had given this task to Ke'in, for the man had well earned this by his actions. That the defenders had good scouting or intelligence was evident; it was only the column composed of Heletaroy's troops which had been thus far attacked. Obviously someone knew they did not have any clansmen with them in large numbers; therefore they used the sort of defense which Aliffa attempted. Some prisoners had been taken, but without exception they proved ignorant of Aliffa's plans. All of them had been outside the hold itself for at least a tenday. When they did find out the composition of the forces marching on Aliffa, they readily consented to return to the fold of Rema. All those who led the attack were sensible enough to know that they could not be trusted, so all who switched allegiance were sent back along the trail to a guarded camp along the main road until the fighting should be over.

They had enough men to do this, for the forecasting of the clan chiefs had been accurate. On the narrow trails and steep vales of the high land there was simply not enough room to construct a large camp—undoubtedly one of the points which had been taken into consideration when the hold was constructed. Now they all saw for themselves the difficulty in taking the hold. Dirshan rejoined the conversation after one last look at the massive hold, coming up as they were all engaged in shaking heads and pursing lips.

"Almost impossible to storm," Snow Leopard was saying as he pointed to the top door. "Rocks would come bounding to take a man with every bounce. As for the door below . . ." He did not have to continue. They had all been watching Dirshan's examination of the lower portal.

"I wonder," Dirshan asked, "if there is some way to the top of the cliff. A trail, perhaps?"

"You are thinking about lines from the top?" Heletaroy commented. "Any man who dropped down would be outthrust by the shape of the cliff there." He pointed to the jutting mass of stone that overhung the hold. "Arrows could pick off a man at leisure. If not, one would have to swing inward to land. That would only put you in a position below the wall itself, and we can get to that deathtrap up the trail."

"I was not thinking of that," Dirshan said. "Think you how they keep warm in there. I see no sign of smoke. It has to come out somewhere, for there are by report some thirteen hundred men in there, along with beasts, women, and other gear. I know that smoke rises, but I see none vented out from yon cliff face. That warren must have some kind of air supply; otherwise all would strangle."

"Yea," affirmed Badger, "but what good does it do us to know that smoke comes out somewhere on the top of the cliff? It would seem to be as useless a knowledge as knowing that the trail we know comes in somewhere to the northeast. Not only is that one hidden, but probably as fortified as the ones here." They had discovered the existence of this other trail from questioning the prisoners they took, but none could lead them to it over the rugged slopes and chasms that knifed deeply to north and east.

"Ah, you are clever," Heletaroy said in admiration. "I, too, noted the absence of smoke, but did not connect it with anything else. Block up those holes and the smoke has nowhere to go but inside that warren. It would make living there difficult. Very good—yes, very good."

"Exactly," Dirshan continued. "I've already sent companies of scouts to look for a way to the top, out of sight of our friends there." He waved to the line of men who watched them from the wall across the valley. "I gave them orders to stop up the holes once they find them. With rock—snow or ice would only melt with the heat. It should soon make Aliffa and those living with him very uncomfortable."

"That will still not get us within the hold itself," Snow Leopard said with finality. "I would not relish climbing yon treacherous path, nor standing below and hacking a way through the lower portal. And I don't foresee Aliffa coming out to treat with us; even if he has moderate sense, he has only to stay within, and the cold will drive us from his doors."

"I have an idea to catch our bandit where the hair is short,"

Dirshan said. "But I will need the cooperation of all, and it is likely that many will die."

"We are yours to command," the others murmured, with heads nodding approval. "We came here to unseat Aliffa. It would mean little to sit here and watch him thumb his nose at us."

"Good. Then continue to build the turtle for an attack on the lower door. It matters little if we breach it, since I think it is backed solidly with stone. But it will provide a diversion for something else. We will meet again tonight, after our scouts return."

They all nodded agreement and went to their separate commands, one leaving to supervise the construction of the large wooden framework, the timbers of which had taken teams of six horses each to drag up the narrow trails. Once set on wheels and dragged up to the lower door, the turtle would provide protection for those men trying to cut their way within. Wet hides would be thrown on top, still green to prevent possible fire from hot oil and torches thrown down by the defenders above. Since this was the most common method of forcing a gate, Dirshan was aware that Aliffa had gathered the means to prevent it, especially since he had the stronghold's great height as an asset. Indeed, one of the first things they had noted about the wall above was a sort of stone ramp mounted directly above the lower door. Imagination was not needed to see where any stones released on it would land.

Light was already gathering into the shadows of late afternoon as Dirshan and Heletaroy made their way back to the tent they shared. It had been necessary to double up as many as possible because of the lack of space; Gett was sleeping with Palcin, though most of the time the Anshani was off arranging for supplies and other material coming up the back trails. Heletaroy had deemed it necessary to keep him away from Dirshan, for already they had had words and there was much tension between them. On the way to the tent, Dirshan deliberately tarried to separate himself and the Anshani from the rest. When they were alone, he paused, turning to stare again at the mass of rock across the narrow vale. "You realize, of course that there is no way that we can take that pile of stone. At least not from the front. The ploy with the smoke will discomfort Aliffa, not drive him forth."

"Of course. I assumed that you had something different in mind, but didn't want to discuss it in front of the others."

"You were right. While I would trust many of them with my life, I still wonder why Aliffa seems to have known all too much about our route, along with how many would come and what was the composition of our forces. I find it curious that only we were attacked, while those who took the other route were spared. Suppose we should be forced to withdraw from this position before that fortress. The massed clans would have lost few men, at little cost in a time of coming reconciliation, whereas my clan and your troops would have lost many. You would eventually be gone from the Range, and the one clan does not matter much against the rest."

"You have clear sight, Dirshan. You should have remained in the Pillars in Alithar. Such talent is wasted here in these rocks. Yet you are right, for there does seem to be the odor of corruption in the situation. And, as you said, there does not seem to be much of a way to enter that hold without a little helpful treachery. I find that unlikely."

"Where there is no speech, there is little chance for treachery. Aliffa has seen to that. Possibly that's why he refuses to talk truce. However, I think we may find another way inside, and without the necessity of someone opening a door.

"Several things have come to my attention that I have not shared with the rest of the clans. The first concerns the men who took an oath not to fight for Aliffa when we were first ambushed on the main road after I met you. All were of the Bears, as you will remember."

"Of course, but they passed west. Our scouts followed them until they were lost in the hills."

"Not all of them. I thought I recognized one at the first meeting of the clan chiefs, for there were some of the Bear clan present when I had to prove clan rights. I ignored it at the time, for then I had other matters to attend to. Yet it seems that three, at least, came east, following in the wake of the rest of us. One came to my tent last night when you were out, offering his services. He claimed to have fought for the Order in Anshan and said he was disgusted with this possible invasion of the Ayal. He had some interesting information which bears on our problem here.

"One: as we already knew, there is a tunnel which leads out of the back of the hold into the northeast. The reason we could not force anyone to tell us where it was is simple: none of them was ever allowed through it. Only selected members of the Bear clan—Aliffa's own—have been so permitted, and that only in the dead of night. This was explained so that none could reveal this hidden escape if captured. A good reason, but it has flaws.

"Those who know how to find the hidden entrance from the outside are few, and the way is guarded by members of the Bears. To gain entrance one has to have the clan sign on the arm and it must be shown. This is how they know that it will not be discovered, for none others have passed except Ayal."

"Does this one know the entrance, then?" Heletaroy asked. "Surely they would have been careful to mask it well. It is only after passing through this rocky waste that I understand the meaning of hidden."

"He does not know the entrance, but he had a clue," Dirshan answered him. "The natural cavern which lies behind those walls above is very extensive; from the living areas to this back door it is some four hours afoot. This gives me some idea of the distance. By sending out scouts to fan the area north and east and using that cliff face as one end of their march and tracing a short arc of a circle it should be possible with some luck to find it. Already Ke'in with his best trackers from my clan are doing this. Others were sent to take care of the smoke holes atop the cliff, using trails we found as they flanked the march."

"Knowledge of this bolthole would be valuable, but did this

one say it could be forced? Though anything would be better than that lower door there—it is a deathtrap."

"He has never seen it in daylight, but better than forcing we shall take it by stealth. Suppose men come in the early morn and simply knock on the door. If they were members of the Bear clan, would they not gain open admittance and take the gate?"

"Possible, if they were members of the Bear clan or we had someone we could trust to do this task for us. Unfortunately, I do not see where these three would do the job for us. They would surely not agree to killing members of their own clan."

"To this the one in my tent agreed, and his clan brothers know nothing of it. But the Bear clan is not the only one to pass through that door. There are also the Ayal—at least some of whom are now within the hold because they have been spotted on the walls. Their guard on the gate does not number over eight to ten men, so this man said, and I think they will not suspect one member of their own clan along with two Ayal bearing possible information for Aliffa."

Heletaroy pulled on his beard, which he had allowed to grow longer in the cold weather, and stared off into the darkling sky of the east. The mountain peaks around them pierced the sky cover. "What is the price which must be paid to assure that this member of the Bears will do as we wish?"

"The head of one of Aliffa's captains. In his rise to power, this one has apparently trampled over many men, one of whom was the uncle to this man, whose name is Seye. He was killed. Seye wants revenge. That and the assurance that he will not have to slay any of his own clan. He wants no possible blood feud if his role is discovered."

"Not an unreasonable request. I assume he wishes to disappear immediately after we gain entrance?"

Dirshan noted the "we" and smiled into the sky. "As quickly as possible. I took the liberty of promising him a liberal amount of the gold from the pouch you keep in the tent, plus two fresh horses. I think he will stay bought."

"Excellent! I applaud your taking advantage of a unique opportunity. Though, of course, if that was one of my own men, I would boil him in fat at the first chance. Still, the workman cannot afford to despise his tools. Who shall go besides you and myself? Or did you intend to tackle the whole fortress with only two men?" There was an ironic tone to Heletaroy's voice.

"Fifty of my Hawks have already started over the trails and have orders to meet us toward dawn. You, Gett, and I will set out later; he is already making us some suitable disguises with the help of Iyali. He has a good eye for such playacting. I think that fifty-some-odd men coming in from behind should be enough to open one of the gates."

Dirshan flexed his back muscles. Cold seeped under the heavy furs he wore. "I shall notify the rest of the clan chiefs before we leave that we have managed to contact a man within, but that he is deciding the price. They will be ready from here should we manage to gain entrance and force a door. But I want no one to alert Aliffa to his danger."

"It is a good plan. It will make excellent reading in my report to Anshan," Heletaroy said. Both men turned to walk to their tent. "It looks like snow again tonight. Let's hope that Ke'in is successful in finding the entrance so we'll be warm tomorrow."

"I agree. I hate to sleep on the rocks in cold."

They set out two hours before dawn. Gett and Heletaroy followed Dirshan, along with one unexpected addition to their small party. This was Iyali, who on Dirshan's return from making diversionary plans with the rest of the clan leaders had confronted him with the statement: "I must go with you. You will need my help if you break through into the hold." She had said it with such conviction that Dirshan had agreed, only warning her that she would have to take the hardship of the journey. He could spare no one to watch over her. To this she said nothing. And so it was a party of four that made its way silently along the back trail until they reached a faint cleft that led vaguely up into the hills. This Dirshan followed without hesitation, and they were soon lost from sight of anyone in the camp below; four dark forms that toiled their way into the cold and barren hills.

Using the subtle markers which his scouts had left behind, Dirshan had no difficulty in following the path. It switched and dipped into the hills and vales, at one time skirting the edge of a chasm so deep in darkness that a rock kicked into it by their passage sent no sound back from the immensity below. Suddenly a form loomed ahead. In a narrow hollow of rock sheltered from the keening east wind, Dirshan spoke with Ke'in, who had awaited their arrival.

"Well," Ke'in said, "the door is found. It is on the other side of this knoll, down in a sheltered valley where a small stream runs. There is a space in the cliff, and gushing from it comes a waterfall that joins the water there. This gave Harl—one of my trackers, and a good one—the first clue, for every other stream this high is already mostly ice. He followed the stream to where this waterfall issued from the rock, and to one side around a rockpile there was a trace of hoof tracks that had been brushed from the snow by branches.

"They led right toward the wall, and then they seemed to disappear entirely. After discovering this, he feigned disinterest and passed on up the valley, for he deemed that there was some way to watch out from the door. I have placed the rest of our men in places here and there around this spot, but they are well hidden from the valley itself. They will be there as soon as the door is opened."

"What of Seye?" Dirshan whispered.

"He waits for you on the other side of the crest, masked by a bend in the valley."

"Good. A fine job of tracking." Then to Heletaroy: "It seems that we shall have some success after all." In the slowly growing light of dawn, he could barely make out the man's form, now veiled in the makeshift costumes of the Ayal. The swirls of blue which had been traced on his face, the beard now gone, made a strange pattern on the man's visage; but in the low light it would pass. Together they left the others on their rocky perch, following the path which Ke'in had indicated down to the place where Seye waited. He was sitting on a rock, staring at the bubbling water which was just becoming visible as it swirled in a pool below him. He started when Dirshan put a hand on his shoulder. After some whispered words to make sure the plans were understood, the three strode up the stream toward the door.

In the early dimness, the stream was only a guide for their feet. They trod lightly as they made their way to the flat cliff face. Spray from the water coming out of the rock made another pattern on their faces as they waited in front of it; nerves made Dirshan stamp noisily in the darkness. Taking the hilt of his blade, Seye beat on what seemed to be a solid stretch of rock. Three times the blade clinked, echoing dully in the cold. There was silence for a moment, and then a warm breath of air seemed to issue from beneath their very feet. Motioning them to one side, he came over to join them. A yawning space seemed to rise from the ground itself, engulfing them with the warm smells of men and horses, doubly noticeable after the thin dry air of the highlands. A warm blot of dead blackness showed itself, where moments before had been the blank face of stone. No light showed within, nor pierced the dark.

"Who comes?" a voice inquired in the hill dialect.

"Seye, of the Bear clan, and two Ayal with messages."

"Advance, Seye, and be known. Let the other two remain outside until we have seen your mark."

Playacting for the benefit of those within, Seye motioned them both to remain while he advanced alone into the blackness. There was a soundless flare, as if a torch had been used in the darkness of a side passage. Then darkness again. Dirshan and his companion waited in silence, wondering if they were being betrayed. Then another command came, this time in the guttural tones of the Ayal language. Assuming that it was a command to enter, the two men loosened the blades which they held naked and concealed under their windblown cloaks and then strode forward into the greater blackness.

The door closed slowly behind them.

XIV

Dirshan, Heletaroy almost treading on his footsteps, pressed
forward into the darkness. The floor beneath their feet was
rock—that he could feel—but for some steps, his outstretched
hand touched nothing, the very blackness of their surroundings
almost palpable, weighing down the air around them. Dirshan
could clearly hear their breathing and the thunder of his own
blood, accelerated now and pounding in his ears. When his
hand finally did come into contact with something, it was with
a comical sense of relief that he gasped.

Some kind of hide curtain had been stretched across the passage opening; Dirshan could make out its doubled thickness.
Moving to one side until he felt the rough walls of the rock
passage, he found that it could be moved to one side. A hiss
directed at Heletaroy brought the other man to him. They
passed behind it as one man. More darkness greeted their
questing eyes, but here the air was even warmer. Groping his
way forward again for another five paces brought Dirshan to another hide curtain. When he twitched this aside, he discovered
that light seeped around his fingers, the wavering glow of
torches that threw shadows against the walls he could barely
make out through the crack.

Knowing that they could not trust their disguises in the sight
of anyone who had ever looked closely at a real Ayal, the two
men had settled on the only workable plan: instant attack. So
it was that after Dirshan jerked aside the last dark curtain and
they were able to enter the passage on the other side they
waited for a moment before rushing forward into one.

A half-vaulted passage stood revealed there, enlarged by man, with the rear portion arching up into what was obviously an extension of the natural cavern where Aliffa's hold was constructed. Five men stood there—six if one counted Seye—and there was an open door to the left through which a stronger light emanated. All the five were armed, one with a cocked crossbow that stood well back. In that instant, Dirshan knew that their ruse had not worked. He could see that the man who had gained them entrance was a prisoner; he was bound, and one man stood close to him with drawn sword and dagger. His face, mouth working futilely, was an expression in fear.

Neither Dirshan nor Heletaroy wasted time in conversation. Jumping to the right in order to get their opponents between them and the man with the cocked crossbow, they attacked.

Dirshan's "For Rema!" screamed and echoed in the chamber as he rushed forward, heedless of the thrusting spear which the closest man held out. Dirshan ducked to the left, and the spear passed harmlessly a finger's breadth from his shoulder. Dirshan knocked it aside as he stood erect and drove the blunted point of his blade into the man's chest. A longsword snaked over his arm to pin the next man in the shoulder even as he withdrew his blade. Heletaroy had come up behind and over Dirshan as he thrust.

Using his mass and speed, Dirshan caromed into the man he had already killed, using him as a shield in order to get closer to the other two men who held swords. A ripping sound followed closely by a high-pitched twang informed Dirshan that the crossbow had been fired, but it was the body of the dead man held before him which took the quarrel. It also took the thrust of his comrade in the back as Dirshan pitched the body up and forward; the fouled sword could not be extracted before Dirshan was up and over to run the crimsoned blade of his sword through the bottom of the man's mouth and into his brain.

In the shouting melee, Dirshan was not sure where Heletaroy had gone, though in the light he watched as the crossbowman began to frantically rewind the string on his weapon. He could do nothing about it, for he was engaged in holding off the fourth man in the chamber—no mean swordsman he, and in full chain mail with a shield. They cut and hacked at each other. Dirshan was forced to give ground even as he tried to keep his opponent between him and the deadly crossbow. This man must have been in command; immediately after beginning the fight, he had backhandedly slid his blade into Seye's belly, dropping him to the ground, and then came for Dirshan. As he was slowly pushed back to the wall, Dirshan looked wildly about the small passage for Heletaroy, knowing that it would be only a matter of a few breaths before a new quarrel, which even as he watched the man was fitting into its guide, should be loosed at him.

Cut and thrust, hack and parry. They danced across the floor. Dirshan slipped twice in the pooled blood on the floor, narrowly dodging an upthrust knife from the man whom Heletaroy had wounded. One hacking thrust ended that danger, but in that moment the man facing him used his shield as a battering ram and slammed it full into Dirshan's chest, throwing him backward and into the rock wall.

His breath was knocked from him by the force of the impact, and Dirshan stood for a second, staring stupidly full into the eyes of the crossbowman. The man's teeth were drawn back in a grimace even as he sighted the weapon and aimed it full into Dirshan's chest. At his shout, the man Dirshan had been fighting jumped back to give him room. In that one instant, Dirshan knew that he was a dead man.

Yet the open mouth of the crossbowman suddenly sprouted wood, a thrown spear passing through to pass into and beyond his neck. Heletaroy had suddenly appeared, grabbing up the spear which had been dropped on the floor and using the opportunity offered by the man's remaining stillness. The swordsman who Dirshan had been fighting was still staring at his dead comrade when Dirshan's blade decapitated him, coming off the wall with such force that the head flew ten feet up the passage. The corpse dropped in a clanging of broken and disjointed metal, blood pumping from the neck.

"You could not have been more timely," Dirshan said with

some strain in his voice. "Were there others?" He motioned with his blade to the open door on the other side.

"Yes, three. When I didn't see the winch here to lower the door, I thought it must have been in there, for they had just lowered it. Your informant there"—he indicated the heap that was what remained of Seye—"was correct. Eight men, eight corpses. As you said, there were four each." There was a smile of satisfaction on his face, and his sword smoked blood on the floor. "Come on in here and lend me your strength. The chains which lift the door as it stands are too heavy to lift alone." He turned and went back into the chamber.

A large room had been carved into the living rock, a kind of combination guard chamber and watch room. To one side was a large wooden wheel girt with heavy chains. Torches were in brackets along the walls, and a table with scraps of food and a half-full jack of wine told what the three men in the room had been doing before they were killed. Dirshan and Heletaroy strained at the wheel, but their combined weight was enough to set it in motion. By some trick of its construction, they could plainly make out the sound of voices above the murmur of flowing water, which only now Dirshan noticed was loud in the chamber. A shaft, concealed from the outside, let in light by which he could see the area in front of the door. There was the clink of steel on stone, and then both men could make out the sound of men moving in the passage between the hide curtains. In order to make it easier, Dirshan went out into the passage and rent the curtain from top to bottom with his blade. Ke'in entered, followed closely by Gett and Iyali, then more and more of the remaining clansmen, overflowing into the chamber and then the passage beyond.

Detailing several to find a place to drag the bodies, the two men walked about the entrance. Stables were found farther back in the caves proper, with fully twenty beasts therein, and huge sections of cavern beyond that were being used at this time for storage for wood and fodder. It was as they returned from examining this that Ke'in came very quickly to Dirshan, a worried look on his face. With him was a younger man, one of the scouts Dirshan had sent out the day before.

The man began to speak immediately. "Hail, O Hawk, and a salute to your victory. But we must swiftly pass within and close the door. The eaters-of-the-dead are coming—they are not far behind me!" With further words he detailed what he had found in his scouting east. In his efforts to find the hidden door, he had stumbled upon a well-worn track leading east, and followed it until he came upon a wide and well-marked road that soon entered a wide valley. Though darkness was almost upon him, there was enough light for him to make out the vast array of men gathered there, with much store of arms and supplies. It was plain that they would move farther in the morn. He had passed several Ayal guards as he approached the camp, and it seemed that they would march to reinforce Aliffa in his hold. "Though the light was failing, I could clearly count ten times two hands of tents and they were large—such as three, maybe four men could use. And farther east, along that road, there were more tents and fires."

"How far away?" Dirshan inquired.

"I ran swiftly, and once off that road, it would be difficult to match my pace on horse. I would say that if they leave this dawn, they will be outside the hidden door here within seven hours—at midday for the forward scouts. I took no one in passing through, so as not to alarm them."

"You did well," Dirshan said, laying his hand on the man's shoulder. "Come to me after the hold is taken. You have earned a good reward for your speed and intelligence.

"Ke'in, I want you to pass outside and bring in all those who remain there. Leave no one outside. Take care that there is no sign outside that would indicate our passage within. I want no warning to the Ayal when they arrive." Ke'in left immediately. The scout followed with a smile on his face.

"I see you have a plan," Heletaroy said to Dirshan.

"Yes, but first we must take the hold. First Aliffa, and if Rema favors us, then the Ayal." They went off to await the incoming men.

Within the space of the sun's final rise outside, they were riding swiftly west through the system of caves, each horse which had been found by the entrance carrying two people. Some fifteen of their men had been left to watch the hidden door, not because Dirshan did not think he would need them at the other end of their dark journey, but because they had no mounts to carry them. Iyali rode with Dirshan, Gett with Heletaroy. Despite his protests, Ke'in had been left in command of the door. Each second horseman in the file of animals carried a torch, both to light their way and give them confidence in a Worlde of drafty darkness.

Though Dirshan had passed through many caves in his time in the Worlde, this one which had been taken over by Aliffa was far the largest. The road that served to carry them was broad—a cart could have passed through the passages without trouble. Indeed, in some time past, this must have been the case, for Dirshan clearly saw the rutted tracks of one beside a damp and soggy pile of rotted sacks. For some reason, Dirshan was sure that use of this cave system had long anteceded their use by Aliffa, and his suspicions were confirmed by passing transparent curtains of slow, flowing stone that coated what was a hand-chiseled surface, laying a tracery of white and crystal that flared and shone in the flickering light of their torches. In that hurrying journey, they passed many side passages and still lakes whose black surfaces spoke of dim depths where black things lurked and hunted, fed and died. Yet Dirshan's sense of urgency was greater than the curiosity that the journey gave him. There was not even time for speech as they passed along the road, for the first few attempts had stirred up ghostly echoes that boomed and reverberated in the hollow passages. By mutual consent, they then passed silently, only the drumming of their horses' hooves giving evidence of their passage.

Dirshan had had a long conversation with Seye on that first night he had come to him and from him had discovered much of the arrangements in Aliffa's hold. It was lucky now that he had done so, as Heletaroy agreed when they had finally settled down in a circle of grave and silent clansmen and explained what each group of men was to do. Their late informant was now a corpse and rested in a side passage with his brothers whom he had betrayed. Heletaroy's only comment had been "saved the gold."

Except for the front portion of Aliffa's hold, where walls had been raised to block off the opening into the cliff, almost all of the area within was on one level. On a hastily drawn map scratched into the dust of the floor, Dirshan detailed the three targets which he thought most important to take when they came to the living areas. He split the remaining men into three groups. Like everyone in the party, he was aware that they were hopelessly outnumbered by the man under Aliffa's command and that if they did not take their objectives in the first rush, they would have no second chance. Gett, with five men at his back, was detailed to take the lower portal, and, once taken, to open it for the entrance of the men who would be waiting outside. Men from their clan and others already knew they were to expect it.

Heletaroy and some twenty-five others were to make for the outer wall, clearing them if possible, but generally making it difficult for the defenders to drop rocks on the gathering clansmen coming up from below. Dirshan and Heletaroy had agreed that it would not be possible to hold the walls for more than a short while once those within the hold knew they were under attack, but that diversion would allow most of the clansmen to enter by the lower door. Cleaning up any resulting pockets of resistance would then be only a matter of time. If they failed to get any more men within the hold, it would not matter to them at all.

For himself, Dirshan selected the hardest task: to enter Aliffa's living quarters, and, if possible, to take him alive. This he had decided on doing alone, above the objections of Heletaroy and Gett; but they knew his argument was sound. The man would be well protected, and an army would have little chance. But one man alone might slip through the darkened corridors. Even Iyali had her task, for Dirshan would not have brought her along if he had not had something for her to do.

She and three men were to find the horses that were stabled some distance back from the actual living quarters of the hold. Once confusion began to spread throughout the hold, Dirshan knew that some would immediately think of escape through the back door; he wanted no heavily armed body of men descending on Ke'in and retaking the portal. The Ayal were coming.

And so they rode in this knowledge, passing in two hours what would have taken them almost five on foot. It was not so much the warmer air or the smells of enclosed humanity which warned Dirshan that they were nearing their goal as he rode at the head of the column. It was the smell of smoke. Those men he had sent above had found the outlets leading upward. Stopping them up had worked, for as they dismounted and left their animals in a deserted side passage, they could see the smoke curl and snake a dirty pattern along the top of the cavern. Those in Aliffa's hold would be uncomfortable this day. Dirshan was pleased.

Outside, the sun was just peeping up over the tops of the hills. The men within the hold awakening to a new day. In the van of the silently moving men, Dirshan came up to the first of the caves where men lived. Motioning to the men behind him to extinguish their torches, he crept forward on hands and knees to peer around a corner. He saw a network of passages, just as described by Seye. A lone man lolled on guard there, sleeping propped on a stool beside a sloping tunnel that led downward. Drawing his dagger, Dirshan slithered forward along the wall, until he was before the sleeping man. Rising to his feet, he kicked the man in the leg, rousing him with a start from some pleasant dream. "Greet Rema!" Dirshan said quietly and then slipped the blade into the man's heart. Dodging the stream of blood which poured out as he withdrew the blade from the thrashing corpse, he lowered it to the floor. Gett and the men under him came forward silently and were motioned to make their way down the sloping corridor. It was the path to the lower door and whatever battle they would find there.

Three other passages radiated from the central passage, one going straight, the other two bending almost immediately once they left the chamber. "Go with Rema," Dirshan said, his head bent to Heletaroy's when the Anshani came up. Heletaroy nodded silently, mouthing the same words, then made his way down the straight and lighted passage. He was followed by the majority of the remaining men, each silently saluting Dirshan as he passed. There was a faint smell of smoke in the air, and torches wavered and danced after their passage.

They stood for a second, Iyali remaining with the three men. "Yours is that way to the stables," he whispered. She nodded, passing close to him and gripping his arm. "Beware of any Ayal wearing white with red swirls on his face," she said in return. "Put on the torque and keep it on. Remember that you cannot fight magic with a sword!" And then she and the others were gone, leaving Dirshan to stand alone in a chamber empty but for a bleeding corpse. He took out the fur-wrapped object in his pouch, fingering it and feeling the coldness even under its covering. Then he removed it from the wrapping and put it on, shrugging it beneath his collar as he did so. It would probably do no practical good, but he did not see where it would do harm. Straightening his clothes and resheathing his blade, an effort to make himself as unnoticeable as possible, he then strode into the passage on the left-hand side of the large chamber.

When Dirshan and Heletaroy had discussed his plans beforehand, Heletaroy had been dead set against Dirshan's attempt. He argued that all their force should be used to take Aliffa, but Dirshan had refused: the hold had to fall quickly, especially in view of the arrival of the Ayal. Thus Dirshan padded alone through the inhabited parts of the hold to find Aliffa before the other was even aware he was stalked. There was a large number of men now known to be living within the hold, of many different backgrounds, and Dirshan hoped to appear as just another renegade—perhaps a tribesman from north or south. One lone man, Dirshan argued, could go in quietly where fifty would encounter nothing but an increasingly stiff fight with no sure result.

That did not make his journey any more comforting. The left-hand path slowly wound upward. Doors opening onto windowless caverns appeared to left and right as he ascended. Dirshan already knew with some rough directions where Aliffa slept—this information from Seye. But it was now well into the morn, and many of the hold's people would be up and stirring. Dirshan expected to run into a few people as he moved around. He was not surprised, therefore, when at a junction of two passages, he came upon another man sitting on a stone under a guttering torch. Though the general level of illumination in the caves was low in any case, Dirshan thought that it was being kept lower because of the eddying smoke that swirled in this higher level. His belief was confirmed when the man said to him as he came up, "Have they found a way to vent off this smoke yet?" the man asked peevishly. "This cave is bad enough when well lit. I'm tired of eating smoke."

"No, but they're working on it," Dirshan replied with a slight smile. "Aliffa still asleep?"

"Naw, he was back and forth here a while ago to use the jakes. Mumbled something about the lousy wine when he passed. A woman was in there with him"—the man leered coarsely and gestured with his thumb—"but she left some time ago. He left orders to be woke as soon as there was food. Guess he wants to go out and look at our freezing friends outside."

"Hmmm," Dirshan mumbled as if to himself. "Well, I had a message, but I won't bother him. It'll keep, 'specially if he's hung over. Is he in the same room? Off the right passage?"

"Naw," the other said, plainly bored with this duty of watching a lifeless corridor. "First hole to the left. Why don't you take a peek in as you go by? If he's awake, then you can report. Like as not, though, he's probably out again. It was pretty bad wine—I had some."

"All right," Dirshan answered casually. He stopped himself from giving the usual "Go with Rema" that was traditional at partings, remembering in time that such beliefs were no longer tolerated here. He bypassed the man, who again leaned against the wall and gazed vacantly around the empty corridor. If things went right, Dirshan thought, the man would soon be fairly active.

Once around the bend in the left corridor, Dirshan willed himself to relax. The tension from his talk with the man had knotted up his shoulders in an unconscious need to ward off a possible blow. There were more torches in this section, and the first door which opened up on the left must look upon a room with even better illumination. A flood of light streamed out into the corridor and created a whiter band across the floor. Walking slowly on tiptoe, Dirshan approached it in silence, poking his head around the entranceway and peering within. His caution was lost. There was no one awake within.

A large room, perhaps ten paces across, greeted his eyes. Three large oil lamps illuminated the room, throwing smoky deposits on the roof overhead and filling the air with an odor of perfumed smoke. Several low tables were placed here and there, some of them with food on small plates and there was more than one empty, tipped stone bottle of wine. A large divan in one corner was strewn with heavy furs, looking more like some shaggy beast than a piece of furniture. Lying across that, on his back with his mouth open and snoring, lay the object of Dirshan's quest.

Dirshan stepped into the room and then across it, in his concentration almost tripping on a goblet which had been tossed or dropped on the floor. Drawing his blade, he put its blunt point beneath the chin of the snoring man, almost gagging from the smell of unwashed man overlaid by the reek of wine fumes that were stronger the closer he came. Then, seeming at this point almost gentle, he shook the drunken man's shoulder. It took several attempts to awaken him. Then there was sudden dawning comprehension in the man's eyes as he stared first at the blade which prevented him from rising and then up at the man looming above him.

"Good morn," Dirshan said in a low voice. "I am Dirshan, leader of the Hawks. And you are Aliffa: outlaw, bandit, and commander of this hold, as well as the man who ordered my father's death. Your enjoyment of life on this side of the Veil depends only on your silence. Am I understood?"

The mute and pleading eyes looked at him over the full black beard. There was more than a lurking fear—nay, there was certainty—that the man knew he would die if he did not do as Dirshan ordered. The bandit's lips formed only the silent word "yes" as he rose, and, following Dirshan's unhurried instructions, prepared to leave his chamber with a sword at his back.

XV

Out of the forty-odd people who entered the living sections of Aliffa's hold, twenty-seven died in the surprise battles. All of them would have, had not Gett, though badly wounded, managed to open the lower doors. There the massed clansmen who had waited, hacking and cutting futilely at the ironclad door, watched it suddenly open before them to disclose a scene of blood and carnage. Sixteen of Aliffa's men died defending it, and four of those who had passed down the passage with Gett had also passed beyond the Veil. Gett and the other clansman remaining held out long enough to operate the winch that separated the stone panels which backed the door, finally fainting from blood loss as the men outside swarmed within. Now both of them rested, along with the other wounded of both sides, in a side cavern tended by some of the women who had been resident within the hold.

Heletaroy had come away unscathed during the sharp fight for control of the walls, though many of his men had fallen. There had been over fifty manning that outer rampart, most of them tipping hot oil and stone on the men attacking the lower portal. They had been taken by surprise, yet after their initial confusion had rallied in the swirling smoke that vented around them and they fought long and hard. There had been no quarter given in that affray, but it was the arrival of the other men pouring in from below into the hold that enabled them to triumph.

Yet in taking the hold, only one Ayal had died, and he by Dirshan's hand. His original purpose in taking Aliffa had not been simply for revenge, though he would take it when the opportunity presented itself. Dirshan wanted to prevent any possible rallying point for Aliffa's men, for though his men outnumbered the defenders, resistance could have been much greater. Aliffa's men had been on home ground, and in the narrow, darkened caverns could have made the taking of the hold thrice as costly as it was. With this in mind, Dirshan had walked the bandit chief—knife concealed in his hand—past the over-friendly guard and farther back into the untenanted portions of the caves. The clash of steel and din of shouted voices grew loud in their ears even as he prodded the shaking man into an alcove. Dirshan had not heeded either Aliffa's rambling threats or his frantic pleas as he stunned him with the pommel of his knife, and left the outlaw there gagged and bound. Then he had passed out looking for battle and found it as he fought his way through the corridors to the outer walls, his own people coming up behind him. Ever and yon he had looked for Ayal, but of all of those known to be within the hold, only the one fell by accident. He had come suddenly out of a side passage and stumbled into Dirshan who was silently waiting around a corner. Dirshan killed him before he realized anything more than that he was an enemy. Of the rest, they could find no trace, though many men were known to have fled into dark places and little-used side passages around the living areas. Even now parties were busy ferreting out those men, though it was a difficult task.

After desperate fighting, the hold was quiet at last, though here and there could be heard the scattered clash of steel as isolated pockets of men refused to take the quarter offered and died rather than be taken. Heletaroy, Iyali, and Dirshan were now sitting in a chamber close to the outer wall. They were all sipping some thin, bitter wine which had been scavenged from one of the storerooms. Men had already been sent above to reopen the smoke passages, and in the thin cold light of late morning they could smell the fresh air that washed out the odor of smoke. Dirshan, one arm bleeding from a cut that was partially scabbed, was wiping the blood from his weapons as Heletaroy spoke.

"Like bees when one breaks a hive!" he exclaimed. " 'Twas brilliant! I swear by Rema I shall give witness to that in An-shan! And there'll be no one to dispute my version of the affair this time!" He referred obliquely to the death of Palcin, who had died after being set upon by four of the defenders. He had long been a thorn in the side of Heletaroy, who knew that he reported his activities to his masters in the Capitol. Heletaroy was not unduly sorry to see him pass beyond the Veil, though he would not have sent him there himself. "The entire hold taken," he continued, "and with the loss of but some sixty men to our side! I will say now that I doubted your plans would work, Dirshan, but this . . . this . . ." He threw up his hands. "And did you see the treasure room? Who'd have believed that that much could have been amassed in such a short time?" That had been the first place Heletaroy had sought when the fighting died down, killing one looter in the process. A strong guard was now posted outside the door to prevent any further activities in that direction.

"That matters not so much to me," Dirshan told him. "I abide by our agreement, and you can distribute most of it as you see fit. Some of it must go as *wergeld* for those that died today, of necessity, or the hills will run with blood from feuds as clan fights clan. I wish no clan wars for the next twenty cycles. Let it end here and be over."

Heletaroy broke in. "Think you that your idea of allowing all those that will agree to fight in the Name their freedom will work?" His voice was filled with scorn. "As soon as we are away, they will find a new leader. Best to kill some to serve as an example."

"No," Dirshan insisted. "I have another idea in mind, one that will confirm them in their newly refound faith even if they do not believe it. Besides, would you have over a thousand men —most of them from these hills—killed? All of them are dis-armed and waiting in the central cavern. Who would kill them, my people or yours? With Aliffa gone, most of them will return to their clans and the ways of my people. It is better so; their strength will be needed in the east."

"Aye," Iyali said. "That is something that we will have to cope with, and soon. I like not that only one Ayal was killed here. With our own eyes we saw two yestereve, and those we have questioned say that there were five within the hold. I wonder where they are now."

"Fled," Heletaroy interjected. "Along with the rest who passed into the back ways when the battle turned against them. It is well you drove off the horses, but they cannot get out. We hold all exits. Even now they are being hunted."

"There is naught we can do about it," Dirshan told them. "This warren has more boltholes than a badger den. Most of them will finally come in as they get hungry. As for the other Ayal, they will have many more of their comrades in these caves if Rema favors us, and those dead. They can stay if they wish and feast upon them."

"I do not think they should be ignored—" Iyali began, only to have her comment cut short by the entrance of one of Heletaroy's men, who was now taking the place of Palcin. "All the horses and men are within," he said at the door. "The men await on your orders."

Dirshan had asked Heletaroy to bring in his animals as soon as it was clear the hold was taken. "Keep the horses saddled and men ready," Heletaroy said to his captain. "We move out shortly. Have each man get a torch from that large storeroom— they will need them on the trip to come." The man left to do his bidding, and Heletaroy turned back to Dirshan. "That part is done. What next?"

"We must gain the help of the Bear clan whose members we have captured. I think they have had time enough to think about their plight now. Let us hope they will help us."

"I think, Dirshan, that sometimes you do things that lack common sense. What hope have you that they will go along with what you propose?"

"Only the knowledge that they are my people. Come."

With that, all three left the chamber and passed through a corridor filled with hurrying men who were preparing the dead and tending the wounded. All nodded respectfully to Dirshan, and there were not a few nods in the direction of the Anshani. Many had seen his battle on the walls. They passed several other side passages until they reached another carven chamber in which five men waited in a huddled knot. Several were bandaged and bore dour looks. They were unarmed and under guard. They looked up apprehensively as Dirshan, followed by the other two, entered the chamber. Dirshan dismissed the guards with a curt "Wait outside" and turned to face the others.

"Who now speaks for the Bears?"

"Aliffa spoke for the Bears, but he cannot be found," one man said bitterly. "I am Liiene, the herald of the Bear clan. You be Dirshan, of the Hawks?"

"Aye, and we have taken your hold. Do you dispute that?"

"No. We have yielded and are fairly beaten. What is your will concerning us? It has been said that you claim clan feud on the Bears for the death of your father. Yet we cannot yield up Aliffa, for none know where he is to be found." Dirshan did not need the other to tell him that they plainly thought that Aliffa had fled during the battle.

Dirshan did not see it necessary to tell him that he still lived, under guard in the camp outside. "That is not the matter I have come to discuss with you. Even now the Ayal are gathering at the eastern door of this cave. What is the feeling of the Bears concerning this alliance between you and them?"

The spokesman looked around, seeming to gather courage from the silent and drawn faces of his companions. "Many would not agree in this choice of an ally, though Aliffa's will was firm in this matter and none could gainsay it. Yet even he did not fully trust them and would never let more than ten at any time within the hold. He distrusted their powers, though he took their counsel and their gold. But I can speak for the clan when I say that most are not warm to this policy and there was much complaint. Clasping a viper to protect against a wolf seems plainly to invite death. But he was clan chief. Now he is gone. Such is the way of Rema, but we have no use for them."

"Good. Then I will offer you a chance to redeem yourselves

in the eyes of Rema and the rest of the clans. This is my offer: Complete quarter and free passage for all those taken in the hold except for those who have been declared outlaw by their clans, subject to two conditions. You must renounce this futile searching for the old gods, for you have seen that they have no power, and return to the fold of Rema. That is the belief that has made our people strong. Second, you must agree to help us fight the Ayal and that this day. We march to the eastern door within the hour. What say you?"

"We must speak on this," the man said and turned to his companions. They walked off to a corner of the stone room. There was the whisper of consultation, and some heated argument. Dirshan and the other two waited in silence as the torch on the wall hissed and burned in its bracket. Then the five men came forward. Their spokesman said, "It would be hard to give up for certain death sworn comrades, even though they be outlawed by their own clans. They have proved faithful to the Bears. Cannot some other arrangement be made in this matter?"

Dirshan made a quick decision. "I will arrange that all those who wish to leave the hold may depart without reprisal, but they must go out the east door once the Ayal are driven off. Their bans will remain in effect, and if they are caught in the Range, it will be on their own heads."

The man nodded in ready agreement. "It is fair. We accept. Your terms are more generous than we had hoped for. How may we help you?"

"Send the others back to your people to spread the word and come with us," Dirshan said. "Time is short and we have much planning to do." As three of the other men left to pass on the word, Dirshan and the rest made plans for the coming ambush.

Within the hour, the hold was a milling mass of men and horses, the stone corridors echoing to the sounds of hurrying feet and voices. A party some thirty strong, most of them members of the Bear clan, had been sent out, riding hard for the eastern door. Their purpose was to relieve Ke'in and take over the manning of the gate from him; some of them had had this duty while Aliffa had the hold and knew the procedure by which the Ayal were allowed admittance. Several of Dirshan's Hawks rode with them to prevent their being attacked. Liiene had guided Dirshan to another chamber where an incomplete map of the caverns was stored, and there they had created the strategy they would use to take the Ayal. Now each party of departing men was guided by a Bear, leading the men to various side passages where they could hide away from the main trail, yet be able to pass out with great speed when the time came.

The last party to leave consisted of some fifty of Heletaroy's men, their commander, and Dirshan. Iyali had demanded the right to be taken along, but Dirshan vetoed it. Her pleas of necessity fell on his deaf ears. Yet her last words lingered with him as they rode into darkness: "You will need my help and I yours, ere this day sees a close, but go with Rema. We will meet again in this fork of the path we all tread." Then her form was lost in the gloom as he strode down the passage, headed for a central point and their station for what was to come.

Their plan was simple, though it needed the cooperation of the Bear clan to work. They had the task of manning the gate, where even then the Ayal were massing. Liiene, who had treated with the Ayal afore, was to act as spokesman and representative of Aliffa and was at the eastern gate already. He was to pass any of the Ayal who wished to enter and split them into groups that were guided by other members of the Bears. Yet this would not be a true guidance, for hidden in the side passages along that road were the massed forces of Anshani and clansmen. Though they did not know exactly how many Ayal would enter, Dirshan had judged that by the time the lead parties reached the midway point from the eastern door to the hold, the majority would be inside the cave system. A strong force of clansmen had been sent out over the mountain trails to cover the door from the outside, reinforcing the men who guarded it and preventing the breakout of any Ayal who might seek to escape. Dirshan had given orders that no prisoners were to be taken, knowing that the hatred the Ayal engendered in his people would be enough to ensure that his orders were followed. He wanted it to be a thorough lesson for them.

Then there was the waiting time, a time of listening in darkness to the silent drip of water and sighing wind. The first of the groups waited in a side passage, its position the closest to the hold itself and the farthest from the eastern portal. With Dirshan and Heletaroy were some hundred men, all trying to be silent in a darkness that seemed to press around them with palpable weight. Even the horses felt the nervousness of their riders; as they listened for the sound of their approaching prey the beasts stamped nervously beneath them. Dirshan gave whispered orders that the men were to dismount and soothe their animals; he wanted no warning given to the Ayal coming into the trap.

They had chosen their position with care. The main trail entered a large cavern and skirted the shore of a deep tarn; the mouth of the cavern where they waited entered this one at an angle and was wide enough to allow two horses to pass abreast. They had all been cautioned to choose and attack their individual targets with care. They would not be carrying lights, and in the coming melee, it was certain that the Ayal would not continue to bear theirs. The noise of their attack was to be the signal for the rest of the men strung up and down the line of caves to attack, too, though they were still to attack swiftly if something went wrong. They would have to trust to surprise and luck—blind luck at that. And yet Dirshan could smell the stink of fear—his as well as others.

Then faintly came the sound of stepping horses from far away, the clink of steel hitting a wall, and the faint and wavering light of windblown torches. From where Dirshan and Heletaroy sat in the van, they could watch the Ayal come up, following the trail around the margin of the dark and silent lake, their reflections passing slowly in double file on the mirrored surface. Dirshan heard the noise as the men behind mounted; it seemed to scream in his ears. Yet the approaching enemy took no notice. Dirshan noted as he picked out his targets that the first members of this party were being guided by Li-iene and that this advance party was garbed in white and rode some paces to the fore. He was reminded what Iyali had warned him about, but in the tension of the moment it simply passed through his mind.

Then the lead party was level with and past the mouth of the hidden passage, their heads never turning, their eyes never moving as they slowly rode past, the patterns on their faces twitching strangely in the torchlight. Dirshan let this first party of some ten pass by before he drew blade, the snick of it clearing the sheath loud in the still air, the sound duplicated up and down the line. Then, using the flat of his blade as a flail, he whipped it across the withers of his horse and it lunged forward. Screaming insanely, the men behind followed, the release of tension a tangible feeling in the air as they rode down to slay their foes.

It was but a moment of breath before Dirshan and the lead attackers were among the Ayal; surprise as complete as the expression of death on the face of the first man he spitted. Then it became a confused melee of shouting men, the scream and cry of wounded horses, and the bobbing of torches still stupidly carried by many of the Ayal. As their men broke through and attacked many points along the line, Dirshan found himself cutting his way toward the front of the mass of men; ducking an outthrust blade, hunching so that a spear passed harmlessly over his head. A horse in front of him reared, braining its rider on a low outcropping of rock, hooves raking a shower of blue sparks as they came down on the walls. Dirshan heard a familiar bellow beside him, turning for a moment to watch Hele-taroy—a captured torch held high in one hand and long blade in the other—cleanly kill one surprised Ayal who froze and watched death ride up, then pin another to his horse as the point went through the man's leg and buried itself deep into the man's saddle.

Then Dirshan's horse reared in panic. One of the unhorsed Ayal had stabbed upward with his blade to get at Dirshan and slipped his blade into the animal instead. Dirshan rode the madly bucking beast down, rolling off as it fell forward to land on his feet. One Ayal tried to ride him down, this time one of those dressed in white. Dirshan moved to one side as the Ayal rode past, grabbed the man's leg, and heaved him out of the saddle. Even above the clash of falling weapons and swearing men, Dirshan could distinctly hear the sound of bones breaking as the man hit the rock floor. Then it was all darkness as the last of the closest torches went down, thrown away as the terrified horseman bolted in fear.

Dirshan found himself afoot in almost total darkness, the wall of the large cave immediately behind him as he put out his hand for guidance. All around was the sound of milling men, the shouts of the wounded, and the shrill whinnies of injured and dying horses. Dirshan knew that some of the Ayal had managed to ride forward toward the living quarters in the hold, and, after orienting himself in the darkness and almost tripping headfirst over a body that lay sprawled and bleeding on the floor beneath him, he stepped over it and began to grope his way up the passage. His hand slid along the wall and gave him a rough guide. As he padded forward cautiously, he came to the passage where the trail left the cavern and proceeded on toward the hold proper.

All was quiet in the darkness; the sound of fighting faded as he went forward. Dirshan walked steadily on. Then suddenly, from a wide bend in the rocky passage, Dirshan made out a faint light that filtered and shone in the blackness. He paused, letting his eyes adjust to it, not liking its strange beauty and compelling feeling that he was being drawn to it. Dirshan flexed his hand on his blade. Something warned him strongly of renewed danger, for that waxing light afore him was not from a torch. As he advanced cautiously, it began to grow brighter with a cold brilliance.

It waxed in strength even as he watched, seeming to pulse like the slow, steady breathing of some gigantic beast. Suddenly Dirshan dropped to his hands and knees, creeping forward to peer around the concealing mass of rock that obscured his vision of the rest of the passage.

It was well that he had done so. Directly around that bend in the wide corridor was the form of a man, his horse and others behind him, the hands gripping the shaft of a tiny ax as he waited for whatever would come around in pursuit. His attention was not directed at the floor of the passage, where Dirshan's head was concealed by an outcropping of stone, and so for some time he was able to see past, up the corridor. What he saw there made his skin crawl and lips draw back in anger.

There was a widening of the passage beyond that created what was in effect a large chamber. Here were gathered five of the white-garbed Ayal. A sixth form—Liiene—was slumped to the floor, staring as if dead at an object which shone with a pulsing brilliance and was the source of the strange light. Because of this Dirshan could not get an exact idea of its shape and fashion, though it seemed to have the outline of an open box of unknown work. But it shone with a light that gripped the mind and pierced the soul, drawing his attention like a war beacon in the blackness. All about it moved the shapes of the five Ayal, murmuring some strange and uncouth cantrap as they moved their hands in obedience to some arcane ritual. Dirshan felt the pull of that light, his mind sucking down the shafts of light that came from it into oblivion.

Shifting his weight to place it more equally on both hands, Dirshan felt a burning sensation on his bare arm that made him flinch away. Looking down, he saw that the torque, which had been hanging unnoticed about his neck during the past day, had now swung free on its chain and almost touched the floor. To his horror, he saw that it, too, now shone with the whitened brilliance of the other object, and it pulsed in rhythm with its fellow across the chamber. And it had grown cold—so cold that its bare touch on his arm had been enough to freeze his flesh with a burn that even now stung him.

A sudden clatter of hooves made Dirshan jerk his attention away from the torque. From the other side of the chamber, where the main trail entered it from the direction of the hold, burst the galloping form of a horse, lather plain on the foam-flecked jaws. Its rider jerked the animal up short even as they

entered, the horses' hooves sliding on the stone as it skidded to
a stop. Yet even as it did so, one of the Ayal reached out with
his hand and touched the beast's head. It slumped to the floor
with no sound, stone dead.

It was only after that quick moment that Dirshan recognized
the rider. It was Iyali. She was now wearing red; a robe deco-
rated with sigils and whorls in brilliant silver, in her hands a
silver wand. Even as her horse slid to the ground, she jumped
off and stood unmoving, her mouth murmuring some incanta-
tion that was not audible to his ears, her wand sketching a
series of intricate passes in front of her in the direction of the
brilliant light.

It was plain that some battle was in the making, for all five
of the other men turned to face her. The light in the chamber
mounted to frightening intensity, the pulse now of a constant
beat, flickering in and out of visual range to blind the eye that
looked directly at it.

Suddenly a wall of almost formless shape and substance
seemed to spring into place between Iyali and the Ayal. Rapid,
darting sparks of great length darted from the object sitting in
the chamber, plainly trying to pierce the shield before Iyali.
There was a sharp smell of burning in the air, a crispness that
tickled the back of the throat. Dirshan watched this silent battle for some time, not knowing how or when he could interfere.
Yet even as he watched, Iyali seemed to falter and stumble.
The formless wall visibly retreated, and the sparks came closer
to the fringes of her red robe.

In that time, Dirshan remembered what Iyali had told him:
that it was not possible to fight magic with a sword. Yet it took
his strength of will to back away from his vantage point and
stand erect. Hefting his blade with one hand, trying to ignore
the searing cold that was seeping through the chain mail from
the torque on his chest, he walked around the bend in the passage in a shuffling crouch. The man standing there died before
he even saw Dirshan; his attention had been focused on the
crackling battle in the chamber beyond. He dropped with a
clank of tumbled metal, the sound unnoticed in the other's in-

tense concentration. Then Dirshan stood in indecision, not knowing what or where he could intervene. Yet even as he paused, Iyali weakened more, and sparks from the shining object came closer and closer to her. One almost touched her shoulder and she flinched aside, rocked by its surging power.

Dirshan began to advance with a slow shuffle toward the group of men, two of whom suddenly transferred their attention to him, looks of dismay plain on their faces. Though many were the bolts that they sent toward him, none seemed to have power as they faded and melted, forced and drawn into the swirling mass of light that had become the torque on his chest. Dirshan was within three paces of the closest man before the first of them fell back as he advanced. Then he suddenly bounded forward, attacking the nearest with the crimsoned tip of his questing sword, dealing blood and carnage in the rocky chamber.

All five of the white-garbed men fell in that chamber of death before the onslaught of his anger, each freezing in transfixed wonder as their spells were powerless over him. The last died even as Dirshan reached over his falling body and swept aside the glittering object—which he could now see was a small box with its top and sides withdrawn—it fell from its rocky perch onto the floor. By some chance of fate or design, the top flipped up and closed, extinguishing the brilliant light. Dirshan turned at that instant to see Iyali, who at that moment slumped to the floor of the chamber.

Then the room was plunged into a blackness as deep as the light which had formerly illuminated it. Even the torque was dark again. Dirshan was left standing in silence, listening to nothing but the sound of blood pounding in his ears.

XVI

It took three days for them to sort out the bits and pieces of that fateful day. Over a thousand of the Ayal had fallen, driven and hunted throughout the dark and bloodstrewn passages of the caves, pursued in the dark places of the Worlde. Of all those who passed through the eastern door that afternoon of taking the hold, none passed outward again to tell his comrades of their fate. It had been the members of Dirshan's clan, passing over the mountain trails to come into the passage from behind, who had sealed their fate. With great loss, they had immediately attacked and driven off the Ayal who remained around the door; these had taken their dead and fled east, beyond the power and might of their enemies.

Many hoped that they would never return, though none knew if that would be true. Yet to be sure the Ayal would never again try to link themselves with any of the clansmen; especially those of the Bear clan, who had lost grievously in that final battle, proving their worth in the darkness. Dirshan was told that at least two of their chieftain-priests had died in that battle of the chamber. Their heads had been removed and set on stakes at the end of the eastern road to serve as warning for any Ayal who might choose to venture west. The rest of the bodies were stripped and left on the slopes for carrion birds and wolves; meat fit only for beasts and things that make their lairs in the ground. There was a mad feasting on the slopes of Muraaz; bones lay mute and white as a warning for many cycles to come, fit remains of a great battle and the destruction of great plans.

Heletaroy had lost two fingers in the battle, which went into the annals as the Battle of the Dark Caves. He fell victim to a berserk Ayal who rushed to his own death in an effort to kill his tormentor. Yet the commander from Anshan was up and moving within the day, his hand a mass of bandages. Thus it was that he acquired a new nickname—Heletaroy the Three-fingered. And it was well that he was up, for his direction was needed in the final days of their victory.

For though it was a victory, it was not one in which they had come away unscathed. Some two hundred had fallen on their own side, dying on the fear-maddened steel of the Ayal. Once they realized that they were trapped, they had fought on in desperation, knowing that they were dead but wanting to take as many with them as possible. They had managed to fall back in some order toward the eastern gate, and only the arrival of the clansmen from behind kept them bottled within. Then had come the last mad, scrambling battle, where friend or foe could only be known by torchlight and hunters fell as often as the hunted. In the end, they all fell, but not before they extracted a price in blood that would long be remembered.

Dirshan had not participated much in that final battle in darkness, for he had been tending Iyali. When he had finally obtained a torch, he had come back to find her almost a corpse, so withered and shrunken were her face and body. He had borne her on his shoulders back to the living portions of the caves and placed her under the charge of two women brought in from outside. It was on the third day that one finally came for him as he tossed restlessly in a darkened chamber. He rose swiftly and followed her to Iyali's bedside.

She was awake, but even to Dirshan's unpracticed eye, she was weakening fast. Taking her hand, he said, "At last you mend. I had despaired that you had already passed into the Veil and would not return."

She smiled wanly at him, fatigue drawing at her eyes. "It is only for this moment, for I have far outlived my allotted span, and this cycle of the Worlde has ended. Yet I go to the next stage knowing that my task is done, and that I have fulfilled what I came to do.

"Do not weep," she continued, clasping his hand. "I knew that this would be my ending here; for even though I could not see the way and shape of that final battle, it has long been known to me the time and hour of my passing. I have finished what I have prepared many cycles to accomplish. Now it is over. If I have any regrets, it is because I know some of what you will see before you, too, come to this end of your path.

"No," she said, reaching up to touch his cheek. "Say nothing, for I would not burden you with foreknowledge. But know you this: that you will see much that even the wise would flinch to view, and there is much good that you will do in the Worlde before you pass beyond the Veil. Rejoice, for your son's sons will not now have to live in fear of what lies in the east."

Iyali paused, her breath coming in short, uneven gasps as if she were under great strain. "The power of the Ayal is broken, for the box and the torque you hold were its symbol and source. Neither can be destroyed by any craft you possess, though you should pass them on to those of more knowledge for safekeeping. I speak of Handlig—he will know how to keep these things and how to rid the Worlde of them. The Ayal will now be destroyed in the way they have lived—by violence and rapine. The power that is in the Order will assure it before many cycles.

"And now . . . now there is naught much else to say. May Rema guide your steps, Dirshan, for in your service you have served the cause of many. May you have safe harbor at journey's end. Farewell . . ."

Iyali closed her eyes. There was a peaceful expression of calm on her face, overlying a look of infinite age and saddened wisdom. Dirshan said naught as he passed from the room, not seeing the line of men who averted their eyes and let him pass silently in his grief.

In later cycles, Dirshan caused a tomb to be built in a high place above the great Vale, of white stone that glittered and shone in the high sunlight of that place. Ever after Iyali was remembered by his people until the memory of her passing and her power was as legendary as the remembrance of his glory.

Then came another time of parting. With the coming of the season of cold, Heletaroy had to pass west again with his men. They stood on a spur of the mountain watching the last of his troops as they waited for their commander, the late-afternoon light gilding the mountaintops about them. Dirshan was standing tensely, nerves strung tight by the duty he had just completed in the vales below. "It was necessary," Heletaroy continued, referring to the fight in front of the clan chiefs in which Dirshan slew Aliffa in front of the assembled men. "You gave him more chance than I would have, for he would have been slowly strangled while boiling in hot oil had it been my father. But it was a fair fight, and none will dispute your right."

Dirshan shrugged, saying nothing as he remembered how the outlaw chief had finally broken and run, falling to his death through his own fear on the mountains below.

"If ever you should pass through Anshan again in your travels," Heletaroy said, "look for me on the Street of Palaces. Some of that gold"—and he patted the saddlebag behind his horse, now loaded with all the jewels he had crammed within, the rest of the treasure on wains guarded by his men—"will not reach the coffers of my good masters in Anshan. Indeed, it shall be *Lord* Heletaroy when next we meet—that is, of course, if gold still has the power to create an ancestry! Go with Rema, Dirshan; I shall cherish the memory of our time together." He saluted him and strode down to mount and ride off with his men, their forms lost in the swirling dust of their departure.

Dirshan's reply, lost in the brisk wind as he watched the man who was now his friend depart, fell into the vales below. Gett had been standing, swathed still in bandages, a little distance away. "Come," Dirshan said to him. "We still have much to do. I would pass away from this high country and seek out the warmer vales."

"Aye, mate," Gett answered. "And I would be well again enough to sample some of the delights which until this time my nurses have only hinted at, but not performed. 'Tis great to be alive and held in honor, is it not?" He chuckled and winked at his companion.

"Aye, Gett. But it is hard to have one without the other."

Saying no more, they passed down the path to the men who waited silently for the return of their chief, and then all passed within the open doors of the hold.